VANESSA PERRY

Wildflowers

First edition

This book was professionally typeset on Reedsy.
Find out more at reedsy.com

To Ryan, my beautiful boy.

Contents

Prologue

My mother and I are dancing in a field of wildflowers. There is a clearing in the middle of the forest, just beyond the creek. We came here often to collect flowers to dry and put up around the house. I loved days like this with Ma. The sun is shining on our cheeks, and we are laughing as butterflies flutter around us. It looks beautiful here, like something out of a fairytale. Occasionally, we caught a glimpse of squirrels playing among the flowers. I can hear birds chirping, and the gentle sound of water flowing through the creek. A spring breeze carries the sweet scent of the wilderness; it smells like fresh grass, mossy woods, and blooming flowers.

Ma was very adamant that we pick only what we would use. "Only take from the land what you need," she reminded me. I held a giant bouquet of Virginia bluebells, black-eyed Susans, and yellow trout lilies. It was the size of my head. The flowers were gorgeous and tickled my senses. I couldn't wait to dry them.

We giggled as Ma asked me if I had any crushes. I didn't. I was more interested in books than boys at this point as an 11 year old. Who needs a boyfriend when you can live in your little world? I loved books so much that I imagine having a used bookstore in town when I grew up.

We finished picking flowers, and we headed to the creek. At the stream, we looked for Indian money. I occasionally shrieked and laughed when I stumbled across a crawdad. They looked like creatures from another planet with their strange tails and little claws. I watched silvery minnows quickly swim by in the clear water. The water glistened, and you could see emerald moss growing on some of the creek stones. We found arrowheads and little fossils. I filled my pockets with them.

I sat alongside the creek and dipped my toes in to feel the coolness of the water. I was barefoot most of the time. The ground feels warm beneath my feet. Ma always said that going barefoot kept you grounded. Ma sat down beside me.

"Let me braid your hair," she said.

Ma braided my hair into two pigtails. Then she made a crown out of dandelions, weaving them together. She placed the crown on my head and said, "See! You are a princess!" Even though I was a little old to be playing as a princess, I still enjoyed the sentiment and couldn't help but giggle.

We sat there for a while, just soaking up the Spring air. And then we just embraced each other in a long, warm hug. Ma wrapped her arms around me and held me close. She felt warm. Ma stroked the back of my hand the way she always did. She said my hands were the softest she had ever felt. We finally got up once the sun started going down.

We headed back to the house and began to work on drying the flowers. We tied them into small bouquets and strung them upside down in the kitchen where they'd dry for a couple of weeks, and they'd be ready to put into vases. I loved the sight of all the little bouquets hanging around the kitchen. It was dreamy.

The flowers that we didn't hang or fell off the stems got pressed into the flower press. I liked putting them in my scrapbook. I used my scrapbook as a lively journal for life's sweetest moments, and I filled it with pressed flowers.

Ma kissed me on the forehead and began to make supper. We had biscuits and gravy for dinner. I always loved breakfast for dinner. Ma showed me how to make biscuits, and I cut them out. She always made the best homemade biscuits I had ever tasted. And she was determined to pass down her recipe.

We ate dinner, and then Ma tucked me into bed. I feel loved and adored. She promised that we would go to the clearing again tomorrow. Then she read me a couple of Little Golden Books to include my favorite- *The Poky Little*

Puppy. I read books for adults now, but I always loved revisiting childhood favorites. It was especially endearing when Ma read to me.

"I love you, Charlotte," she said.

"I love you, too, Ma," I replied.

Then we proceeded with our bedtime ritual of Eskimo kisses. It was a wonderful day.

Chapter 1

"Charlotte! Charlotte! I want some cereal!" Anna said. I woke up to see her sweet face all cross-eyed as she giggled. The sun was shining through my bedroom window. Birds were chirping. The trees were swaying in the winter breeze. I yawned and stretched my arms. I made my way out of my twin size bed to get breakfast made. The wooden bedframe creaked as I plopped my feet down onto my furry cream rug. It felt soft beneath me. I was ready to seize the day.

I yanked an aqua green t-shirt over my head and slid into my favorite pair of jeans. Today was Ma's birthday and I was so excited that I felt an internal buzzing. It would be a great day.

"Today is Ma's birthday," I told Sadie and Anna. "We're going to make her a strawberry cake with strawberry icing."

Sadie's eyes lit up and sparkled. I think she was just as excited as I was. I poured the girls each a bowl of Fruit Loops. They gobbled them down quickly. I thought about how Daddy used to love Fruit Loops so I poured myself a bowl. I loved the sweet, fruity scent.

"When are we baking Ma's cake?" Sadie asked.

"As soon as we clean up your room today," I said. "Something in there reeks!"

As I did every morning, I brewed Ma a fresh pot of coffee. I poured her a cup and watched as the steam swirled into the air. I added three spoons of sugar and just enough hazelnut creamer to lighten the coffee a little. I took a small sip to taste test. It was just like Ma liked it.

I carefully carried her cup to her room. I knocked, but she didn't answer. It was typical for her to be still asleep when we girls woke up. I opened the door and was delighted by all the sunlight bouncing off her extensive collection of crystals that filled an entire bookshelf. They glistened in the light like giant chunks of glitter. There was amethyst, quartz, emeralds, and even more crystals that I didn't know the name of.

Ma had always collected crystals. She had told me when I was younger that they were good for protection and healing. I no longer see her using them but I remember her using them frequently before Daddy died.

I ran my hand over a vase full of dried wildflowers. We hadn't picked flowers in years. But Ma had insisted on keeping these old ones in her room. Despite being a couple of years old, they still were in mint condition for dried flowers, though they appeared fragile, as though one wrong move could break the petals from their stems. The wildflowers remind me of happier times with Ma.

Mauve lace curtains hung on the windows. Another bookshelf filled with novels sat in the corner next to Ma's faded maroon reading recliner. She also had porcelain angel knick knacks on the shelf. Houseplants hung from the ceiling.

I looked over at Ma. She looked so peaceful when she slept. When she was awake, she was always frowning with her brows pushed together. But now, her face was relaxed.

She looked like a gracefully aging 30-year-old. Her auburn hair was warmth on a cold winter day, as was her olive, tan skin. I wish that I had her olive skin, but mine was pale white like Daddy's. I was built like Ma, though. She was of average height and had a girlish, slinky figure.

"Ma, I got your coffee." I shook her gently. Her deep hazel eyes looked up at me wearily. "Happy birthday, Ma," I quickly said before she could protest me waking her up. She slightly grinned and then asked, "Are the girls up yet? Have they been fed?" Ma never smiled, so that was a good sign.

"Yes, they had cereal. Can the girls come in?" I asked.

"Give me a few, Charlotte," she said as she sat up to drink her coffee and light a cigarette. "Also, empty the ashtray for me."

I wasn't sure if Ma was what people called a chain smoker, but it sure seemed like it. I always wondered how she managed to age so well but smoke so much. It was clear she smoked like a freight train. Yet the only wrinkling starting to show was between her brows. I hoped that I had the same genes as Ma so that I could age just as well.

I emptied the ashtray while holding my nose from the scent and then left her room. It was time to get some things done. Oh, yeah. The rotting meat smell in the kids' room needed to be taken care of. I dreaded finding whatever it was that was causing the smell.

I entered the kids' room, where toys were strewn everywhere. Barbies, stuffed animals, and crayons littered the floor. I began to pick up but noticed that whatever smell was there last night was already gone. Instead, it smelled of markers and crayons as usual. Still, it was time to tidy up the place. I drew back the long pink curtains to let the sunlight in and noticed a crow sitting on top of the mailbox. Ma said crows were good luck and that they were intelligent creatures that deserved some respect. She said that they could even remember people, so it was best to be fair to them. So, I waved at the crow until it flew away.

I hollered for the girls to come to help me clean up. It was their mess, after all. Although they were reluctant to help, they finally got into the mood when I started singing.

"Clean up, clean up. Everybody everywhere. Clean up, clean up. Everybody do your share." I would sing faster and faster as Sadie and Anna picked up their toys and laughed hysterically. "See, girls! Cleaning doesn't have to be boring!" I said as I laughed.

I told Anna to get the vacuum and Sadie to get the mop. As Anna came back with the vacuum, her auburn curls bounced behind her. She was adorable and still had baby fat and plump cheeks as a five-year-old. Her skin was olive toned like Ma's, but Anna's face was spotted with freckles.

"Can we bake the cake now?" Sadie asked.

"It is noon, so I guess that is late enough," I told her.

We headed into the kitchen. The kitchen, while daunting to clean, was one of my favorite places to be. The mint green cabinets against the cream-colored walls transported me back in time. I loved the big kitchen island in the middle, even though it was old and needed a fresh paint coat. Even the floors looked different in the sunlight with their dark oak color. Hopefully, Ma never got up the energy to change the kitchen like she had been planning for months. I thought it was the perfect cottage core look. However, maybe I was just in a better mood. At night, when I had to mop the floor, I despised the floorboards.

I grabbed our most enormous mixing bowl and our old handheld mixer, and two circular pans for the cake. I got the cake mix. I let the girls break the eggs and mix the batter. After pouring the batter into the pan, they began to fight about who would get to lick the spoon. So I gave Sadie the spoon and Anna the bowl and let them have it. They each had pink cake batter strewn all over their shirts, and they looked as sweet as ever.

It brought back memories of baking with Ma. Strawberry cake was her favorite so we used to bake it often. Ma taught me how to measure ingredients and how to make sure the cake was perfectly done. She used to give me the spoon to lick.

Soon, the scent of strawberry cake began to fill the kitchen. Once done, the girls helped me ice the cake with pink strawberry icing as promised. The girls insisted on adding sprinkles, so I let them put a few too many white sprinkles on top. We settled with putting 30 individual candles on the cake. I lit them, thinking that the cake would surely go up in flames, and we carried it to Ma's bedroom.

We sang Happy Birthday to her, and I think it was the happiest I had seen her since Daddy died. She was smiling from ear to ear. I realized how much more youthful and carefree she looked when she smiled. And for once, Sadie looked relaxed and happy to be in Ma's presence. The cake had worked.

She said thank you and asked me to cut her a piece. So I took the cake back into the kitchen, where I cut pieces for everyone. I was so glad that today would be a good day.

I took Ma her piece and asked if she would be joining us. "I'll just eat it in my room Charlotte," she said unsurprisingly. "Did you clean the girls' room today?"

"Yes, Ma. Last night there was a weird, nasty smell in there. It smelled like rotting meat. But it was gone today, and when we cleaned, I didn't find anything out of the ordinary," I told her. "And trust me, we cleaned their room from top to bottom."

Ma looked at me with a nervous kind of look. I thought she was going to get mad about something. Instead, she sighed and said, "Why don't you have a movie day with the girls after you clean the bathroom."

"Okay. I love you, Ma." She looked a little surprised as I hardly said those three words anymore. But I figured it was appropriate with it being her birthday and all. She didn't say it back, but she gave me a half-grin. That was good enough for me.

While Ma seemed to be in a good mood, I was still a little hurt that she'd be spending the day in her room again. She was rarely in a good mood anymore so I would take it for what it is. Nonetheless, I began to clean the bathroom. The porcelain tub with the claw feet was my favorite. It was great for soaking in a long hot bath. The white tiles that filled the bathroom, on the other hand, were the bane of my existence when it came to cleaning. The grout was hard to keep clean, and the white tiles showed every bit of any mess left behind. I scrubbed and scrubbed and scrubbed while I thought about Daddy.

Daddy had put the white tiles in the bathroom himself for Ma. I remember how proud he was when he had completed the project. It made Ma so happy, too, and I think that's what made Daddy the happiest. Whenever Ma was gleaming with happiness, Daddy was in the best mood in the world. Everything Daddy did was for Ma and his family.

I finished cleaning up the bathroom and was quite happy with the way it turned out. The white tile was glistening in the sunlight. It smelled of cleaning products, and I loved that citrusy clean smell. The golden tub and sink fixtures were shining. And I had laid out a clean beige rug beside the tub.

While I cleaned, the girls did their school work; we were homeschooled. We weren't always homeschooled. We started after Daddy died. Ma said that it was the best way to make sure she could raise us how she wanted to. But

I think she initially had a fear of letting us out of her sight and something happening to one of us. The girls and I have excelled since homeschooling. We were able to learn at our own pace, so we were ahead in most areas.

At first, I was excited about homeschooling. I wasn't fond of public school. I had no interest in making friends at school or finding a click of people to fit into it. I mostly focused on my studies because Ma put such a big emphasis on learning. Also, with homeschooling, I was able to study what I wanted. If I wanted to learn a new language, I could do it. However, I was missing school these days because I wish that I could have a break from Ma, taking care of the house, and looking after the girls.

I headed to the living room. It was already clean as I cleaned it daily. I closed the long white lace curtains to get ready for the movie day. I took the cushions off our green, floral couch. I made a pallet on the floor. I moved the family Bible from the coffee table so it wouldn't get ruined between Anna and Sadie, placing drinks up there and everything else. A picture of some woman fell out. It was in black and white, and she was wearing a hat with a wide brim. She looked enchanting. The back read, "Aunt Em- Ut supra, sic beow." I had no idea what that meant, but Aunt Em was my great-aunt. She lived in Maine. I didn't know much about her except that she had moved to Maine for a teaching job. Our family lives all over the country now. We had once been close but everyone moved away to pursue their own dreams.

I was flipping through the Bible and noticed writing in Latin along with strange symbols. Some of the Latin writing seemed to be a recipe as it had what appeared to be measurements and a list of ingredients but I couldn't be sure. I hadn't flipped through the family Bible since I was a little girl so I didn't remember any of these things. I wondered what they were for.

Ma was passing through the living room and she stopped abruptly.

"Charlotte, put the Bible away. I don't want you meddling in it," she said firmly.

"But Ma I just wanted to look through it," I said. "Why is there Latin in the Bible?"

"Don't ask me questions," Ma said with a stern look on her face. "Put it away and don't meddle in it again."

I put the family Bible away, and I hollered for the girls," Sadie! Anna! Movie day!!" They came running into the living room. The movie day was always fun. I poured all of us some grape Kool-Aid. It smelled like candy. And we popped some buttery popcorn. You would think it would be hard to settle on movies with the three of us, but we had a system. The youngest picked the first movie. Of course, Anna picked Hercules. Then Sadie picked Snow White. I chose Cinderella. We had a lot of fun singing along to the movies and reciting lines on the living room floor. The girls had beautiful voices that sounded like singing angels.

The phone rang.

"Hello?" I answered.

"Hey, Charlotte, it's Aunt Cindy," replied the voice on the other line.

"Aunt Cindy!" I exclaimed.

"How are you?" she asked.

I told Aunt Cindy all about Ma's birthday cake and then she asked to speak to Ma. So, I hollered for Ma to pick up the phone from her room.

Aunt Cindy was Ma's younger sister. She was an actress trying to make it big in California. Ma was always excited to hear from Aunt Cindy.

It was time for me to cook dinner. I chose the first meal that Ma ever taught me to cook- Tuna Surprise. It was merely mac'n'cheese, tuna, and peas mixed. Ma had led me to make it when I was only seven. It was a household favorite with it's cheesy taste. And I knew that it would be a great ending to a pretty good day.

We ate dinner, and I cleaned the kitchen. I washed the dishes. The water was warm and soapy and smelled clean. I carefully scrubbed each dish and watched the occasional bubble float up from the sink. Before I could finish, Anna asked me to lay with her so she could go to sleep. So, I did. Before long, I was asleep myself.

Chapter 2

WHACK!

The hard remote met my forehead with a sting, and I was startled awake. I already knew why Ma had woken me up. I had fallen asleep without mopping the kitchen floor again. Falling asleep without cleaning the kitchen was happening a little too often lately for Ma's liking. I quickly got out of my sister's bed and made my way to the kitchen.

As I flipped the light on, I looked around the kitchen. Roaches were scurrying back to their hiding places. They always came out at night, no matter how clean I kept the house. Little scavengers were looking for any bit of crumbs, although I made sure never to leave any behind. I think they came with the territory. Our house was nestled deep into the woods in a small town called Billington.

"Hurry the fuck up and stop daydreaming, dumbass!" my mother yelled.

I replied quickly, "Yes, ma'am."

I began mopping the floor, as I did every night. The only reason I had fallen asleep is that Anna was terrified of the dark and insisted I lay with her until she fell asleep. I didn't mind lying with her. It was just that I felt drained tonight. Plus, she insisted on cuddling. She claimed that if you weren't facing her that you weren't lying with her.

"You know, if you did this before putting the kids to bed, you'd be asleep right now, Charlotte." Ma said flatly.

As much as I wanted to tell her that she should put her kids to bed instead of her 13-year-old daughter, I kept quiet and focused on the old wooden floorboards. Back-talk meant a back-handed slap to the mouth in this house. I carefully mopped the floors, making sure I didn't miss a single spot. The water sloshed against the floorboards with tiny bubbles forming on the surface. Mop, rinse, repeat.

"Make sure you mop it real good," Ma said.

Of course, I would mop it well. If I did not, Ma would make me clean it again. And I was just ready to get to bed. I had bags under my eyes and my head ached. I couldn't stop yawning. The girls had woken me up early, again.

Ma left to go back to her bedroom without saying another word. She stayed in there most of the time watching Soap operas on TV or reading romance novels. Whenever she left, so did the tension in the air. There was always tension in the air when Ma was around. It was like walking on eggshells. You never knew what would set her off. Sometimes, I felt that if I breathed wrong that she would get mad. With Ma gone, I breathed a little deeper and my shoulders relaxed. I thought about the first time Ma ever hit me.

We stayed at my grandmother's house after Daddy died, and I guess Ma was stressed with work. She was a Registered Nurse then working in a retirement home for the elderly. We were hanging up clothes, and when I failed to work fast enough, Ma hit me a few times with a coat hanger. I remember crying uncontrollably as my mother told me she was sorry. I will never forget that day. It's not that it hurt particularly bad- though it did hurt. Before then, however, Ma had never laid a hand on me.

Ma didn't turn to physical punishment for a while after that. I thought maybe Ma was just having a bad day. I am still not sure why she did it. But I do know that after that, I was always quick to hang the laundry. Still, Ma was certainly adamant that the best form of punishment these days was physical punishment.

I finished mopping, only to be displeased. Mops can only do so much for the cold, old wooden floor in this house. It was scuffed and scratched, and it needed to be updated badly. Ma said its antiqueness added to the charm of our cottage home, though. Plus, our family passed our home down through generations, and Ma thought the floors represented the foundation laid by family members long passed. I headed to my room with a yawn where I could find solstice and hopefully dream of brighter days.

"Charlotte, there are people in my room," Sadie said as she woke me up.

"There is nobody in your room, kiddo," I told her sleepily. I walked her back to her room. She stumbled along with her long, black ponytail swaying with her. Her pale skin glistened in the moonlight. Sadie is petite for a seven-year-old. She looks like a life size porcelain doll.

My bare feet were cold against the floor. It seemed a little chillier than usual in the house despite the thermostat always set at 70. Ma forbid anybody from touching it, so I would just have to bundle up tonight.

The room was cluttered with toys but aside from Anna sleeping in her bed, it was empty. A teddy bear rested in their old rocking chair and I promptly moved it because it looked a little creepy in the dark.

"See. There's nobody here," I reassured her.

"Nobody here except the smell of days-old meat," I thought to myself. Phew! What *was* that smell? And why was it back? I looked around the room for a culprit, but I couldn't see anything in the dark. And I didn't want to turn the light on to wake Anna.

"Yes, there was. The people were dressed up for a wedding. I saw them," she insisted.

I tucked her into bed and told her firmly, "Next time, you should wake up, Ma. It was just a dream."

"CHARLOTTE. It was not a dream. I saw them," she said as she rubbed the back of her neck. "A woman was wearing a wedding dress. She had a big bunch of flowers. And there were other people in dresses and suits."

I rolled my eyes and yawned, "Sadie, I promise you that it was just a dream. Now go back to sleep."

Sadie always has had a big imagination. It was almost as if she started telling stories as soon as she could talk. And you could hardly believe a word Sadie said. The girl told so many fibs that it was as if something were wrong with her when she told the truth. And since Daddy died, a year ago, the lying had only gotten worse. I was sure that tonight was absolutely no exception. She often lied to try to stay out of trouble or told white lies to get attention. One time, she even said Anna stole the money from her piggy bank and we found the money under Sadie's pillow.

13

"I know it wasn't a dream, and you won't believe me," Sadie said.

"If you are scared, you can sleep in my room tonight, but I am going back to bed," I said.

Sadie replied, "Charlotte, I wasn't scared. I just want you to believe me. They were here."

"Okay, Sadie," I said. "Well, goodnight. Now get some rest."

"Goodnight," she said hesitantly.

I went back to my room to go back to bed. But for the rest of the night, I was restless. I grabbed my father's pocket watch from my nightstand to check the time. It was 11:15 PM. I held the silver watch in my hands and rubbed my thumb over the engravings. I missed Daddy so much.

Daddy had died a year ago. He passed away peacefully in his sleep; the doctors said his heart just stopped. I held the watch close to my heart as I listened to the ticking and let it soothe me.

Ma stopped by my bedroom door.

"Did you finish the kitchen?" she asked.

"Yes, ma'am," I replied.

Ma left as abruptly as she had come.

When Daddy died, it was like a colossal piece of Ma died, too. She had become depressed and quiet, initially. Then Ma started staying in her room more and more. It seemed the less she came out, the angrier about the world she was. Even then, things had been especially rough lately. You truly never knew what was going to make Ma upset. And we hardly ever saw her without a frown. It was like she was utterly broken. She was a shell of what she used to be.

I sighed as I pulled out an Anne Rice novel from my bedside nightstand. I had been reading adult novels since I was eleven. Ma said that I was ready for them and she took reading very seriously. She told me that reading helped expand our minds.

After a little while, I shut my bedside lamp off and finally drifted off to sleep. This time, I was dreaming of wildflowers— beautiful, fragrant wildflowers filling my room to be dried.

Chapter 3

I was brushing my long, raven-black hair when I noticed I was losing hair again. There were strands upon strands in my brush. Unfortunately, it was a side effect of stress, according to Ma. Of course, she didn't understand what a 13-year-old could be stressed about. I sighed and set my brush down. Ma had made me a concoction of olive oil, tea tree oil, and lavender oil to help me with hair loss. I didn't think it had been working. I had been using it for about six months. But she insisted that I just had to stick with it. So, I rubbed some in the palm of my hands and applied it to my roots. Ma said she wasn't having a ratty-looking daughter. I headed to the kitchen to make chocolate chip pancakes for the girls.

I stepped on a Barbie shoe in the hallway, which is undoubtedly more painful than stepping on a LEGO. I would rather stub my toe on a pitchfork. I yelled for the girls to pick up their mess at once. The girls littered the floor with Barbie's clothes and other toys. I worked too hard to keep the house pristine so that Ma wouldn't make a fuss about it. The least they could do was keep their mess in their room.

In the kitchen, I realized Ma had already made her morning coffee. It smelled of freshly brewed coffee, and the pot was half full. That was a bit unusual, but she did make it herself if she were up before me, though that was rarely the case. I gathered pancake mix and chocolate chips. I began to make the fluffiest, buttermilk chocolate chip pancakes in the world, aside from grandma's. I missed Grandma much, and cooking always reminded me of her. Much like Ma used to, Grandma always let me help in the kitchen. She taught me how to cook many things before Daddy died. Those were memories that I held dear to my heart. But Ma and grandma had a falling out some time ago, so we hadn't seen her in a year. I wasn't even sure what they were mad at each other over. But they had yelled and argued about religion and something about losing those you love.

Sadie and Anna came running in to investigate the aroma of breakfast. "Pancakes!" they exclaimed in unison. It smelled of pancake batter, warm butter, and syrup. They ate them as fast as I could make them. I chuckled to myself over how quick and how much two tiny girls could eat. It was a beautiful sight to see the two girls getting along at our old, wooden kitchen table. They loved when I cooked. Unfortunately, they didn't have an interest in learning how to cook themselves. I had learned some essential recipes at their age. But Ma didn't cook much anymore, so I was the only one that could teach them even if they were interested. And, truthfully, I preferred cooking without anyone in the way anyway.

"Alright, girls! Let's get dressed and spend some time enjoying the weather today," I told them. In the blink of an eye, they were dressed and waiting at the door for me to come to join them. Sadie wore an old blue church dress. She always liked dressing up. She looked much like me. We both have black hair, gray eyes, and pale skin like Daddy did. Anna dressed in mismatched clothes. She wore a bright pink top and green leggings. She loved to dress like a peacock, it seemed. Anna looked more like Ma. She had the same auburn hair and hazel eyes. And her skin was more of an olive tone. Both of the girls were gorgeous in their ways.

We spent much of the day outside. It was beautiful for a winter day. This winter had been particularly harsh with power outages. Some townsfolk had passed away from carbon monoxide poisoning as they tried to stay warm with gas heaters in their home. Every day was bone chilling cold with grey skies.

But today wasn't too cold, and the sun was shining for once. You could smell the woods and hear the creek in the distance. We played tag and rode our bikes. The girls were always happiest outside, where they could run and be the little wildlings they were. They were beaming with happiness as they smiled hugely. The sound of them giggling filled the air. As long as the girls were delighted, I was also pleased. I enjoyed spending time with them. They always made my day just a bit more special. And I loved nothing more than to be outside. The fresh air and open sky always made me feel free.

We decided to listen to some music on our balcony. Britney Spears and N'SYNC played on our radio, and we sang along gleefully. The kids asked me questions about trees and the sky, and I answered the best that I could. We talked about the forest. We chatted about movies. We read jokes from an old joke book that I had, and we laughed a lot. It reminded me of Ma and how she used to sit outside with us and engage in conversation. I missed her.

"What did the big flower say to the little flower?" I asked.

"I don't know," the girls said in anticipation.

"Hi, bud!" I exclaimed.

We all giggled. It seemed that the girls were little jokesters like Daddy was. They were always telling jokes and asking me to tell them jokes. They even loved to prank one another though I was a bit more momentous like Ma and didn't want to be included in those shenanigans.

Anna decided to slip through the railing of the 9-foot balcony and walk around it from the other side like she always did. Anna was still doing stunts since the time she could walk. "Anna, please be careful," I cautioned her. Sadie and I weren't quite as daring, so we looked at her nervously. Anna had discovered she could slip through the railing last summer. She nearly gave Ma a heart attack when she threatened to try to fly. Now, any time we are on the balcony she just can't seem to stay on the safe side of the railing.

Sadie and I were casually chatting about homeschool work. She wanted to study elephants, her favorite animal, next. But that was certainly not in the curriculum. However, I did agree that we'd do some research in Ma's old encyclopedia set as an extra-curricular. Suddenly, as we were talking, the air became still with the birds' sound chirping ceasing. Then, a breeze blew through my hair, and that's when I saw Anna fly backward off the balcony.

I scrambled to my feet and ran down the stairs as fast as I possibly could. "Anna, are you okay?!" I yelled. I pulled her from the rose bushes at the foot of the balcony. Aside from being a little banged up and scratched by rose thorns, she was okay. Still, I think she was so startled she had wet herself and was sobbing.

"What happened?!" Ma yelled as she flung the door open.

"Anna was walking around the balcony railing again, and she fell," I said.

"No! I felt Sadie push me!!" Anna told Ma.

I defended Sadie, "Sadie was on the stairs the entire time nowhere near Anna!"

SMACK.

Ma slapped me hard across the face. It stung so bad that I was in shock. Tears ran down my cheeks. I was speechless. I felt dizzy and my arms felt numb. Ma's face was beet red and her eyes seemed to bulge. Sadie began to cry hysterically. Anna looked shocked, even though she was still sobbing.

"YOU are supposed to be watching the girls! If you were watching them, this wouldn't have happened! You are lucky she isn't hurt any more than she is!" Ma yelled as she pulled up the sleeves to her shirt. "And Sadie, I am going to beat your ass for pushing your sister."

"But, Sadie didn't do anything!" I pleaded to Ma while biting at my lips.

Ma pushed me as hard as she could, and I fell backward into the rose bush.

"I have told you not to back-talk! But since you think Sadie doesn't deserve to be punished, then you can deal with it," Ma told me angrily.

She picked up Anna and carried her up the stairs. Anna sobbed loudly in her arms. Sadie came running down to ask if I was alright. I was except for the thorns that had torn skin on my arms and hands. I went inside to clean myself. Sadie followed along. I felt awful for her as she did nothing wrong, and she didn't deserve to be blamed for Anna falling.

The water stung as I washed my skin. Blood pooled in the white porcelain sink. I was crying quietly to myself as I wondered why I deserved to be treated this way. Then, I began to think, once again, that I would be better off dead. I started imagining what it would be like to slit my wrists while in the tub and calmly watch blood spill out into the bathwater. I imagined a pool of crimson swirling around me. Would I slowly drift off to sleep? I thought that everything would just slowly fade to black. It seemed so peaceful. But I couldn't leave the girls behind. Lord knows that Sadie would take my role, and nobody would be here to defend her. She would be in charge of taking care of Anna and the house, and no child needed that much stress.

I finished cleaning myself up with the help of Sadie handing me a towel, and I pulled myself together as I did every time Ma lashed out. There was no use in crying about it further. What was done was done. I wanted to do something therapeutic such as paint or draw but I had to get ready to make dinner. Tonight I was making hamburger helper. I could only stand it a little bit, but the girls loved it. Ma didn't care for it much either, but she would eat just about anything I cooked.

At the dinner table, the girls acted as if nothing had even happened today. They giggled about how much butter should go on their bread and who could make the loudest slurping noise by practically inhaling their food. I turned to Anna and said, "Listen. I am sorry that you fell today, but I want you to know that Sadie didn't push you. She was on the stairs the whole time."

"But *somebody* pushed me, Charlotte. I felt it." Anna insisted.

I wasn't sure what to think. Sadie told tall tales a lot, but Anna never lied. She never even said the tiniest of fibs. I was thinking about the people Sadie said she saw and Anna claiming to be pushed gave me chills. Perhaps the breeze had startled her, and she had fallen. She was probably so scared that it happened a little differently than she realized. However, the way she flew backward almost looked as though somebody pushed her, and the breeze hadn't been that strong.

The girls finished eating then they started bickering.

"See. I told you that I didn't push you," Sadie said.

"Well, if you didn't, then who did Sadie," Anna rebutted.

"Alright, girls. Alright. We aren't arguing about this, much less even talking about it anymore. Enough is enough. Go put on your PJ's and hang out in your room so I can get this kitchen cleaned," I instructed them.

I began clearing off the table when Ma came in. "So you still want to tell me that Sadie didn't push Anna?" she asked.

"Ma. I did not see Sadie push Anna." I said calmly.

"You didn't see it because you weren't paying attention," she said flatly.

I said, "Yes, ma'am." And I left it at that. There was no arguing with Ma. There was no disagreeing with her. And, frankly, I had chores to get done anyway.

I washed the dishes using bleach water. Despite the dish soap specifically mentioning not using bleach, Ma insisted that it was the only way to kill germs. The scent stung my nose and the bleach made my skin tingle. I swept and mopped the floors and I cleaned the counters and table, carefully sweeping crumbs into the palm of my hand. I thought about how Daddy and Ma used to clean the kitchen together after dinner. Ma would wash the dishes and Daddy would do the rest. They used to do everything together.

I headed to bed. As I was getting dressed, I looked at the scar on my cheek. It was a scar from when Ma had slapped me once several months ago, and her wedding ring caught my skin. The funny thing is that I don't even remember why I got beaten anymore. I just remember that Ma had left me to attend to my wound myself. I hated that scar. It reminded me of the person that Ma has become. But with time, it was getting lighter and lighter, so I hope that one day it will be gone altogether.

Chapter 4

Ma was drinking her coffee in the kitchen the following morning. "Good morning, Charlotte," she said with a crisp nod.

"Good morning, Ma," I replied. I felt a heaviness in my stomach. I tried to gauge whether or not she was in a good mood.

"Charlotte, I need to talk to you about something," she said. Her head was cocked slightly to the side.

"Sure, Ma. What is it?" I was wary, but my curiosity peaked. I felt my shoulders tense. Ma hardly *talked* to me.

"I know things have been rough around here since your Daddy died," Ma said. "And I am sorry that you have had to pick up on a lot of the slack around here. It's just been hard since he passed, and I have let it get to me for too long. I will start doing better."

"Ma, it's okay," I said. I didn't really mean it, though. It wasn't okay. But I'd say anything to try to have a good day.

"No, it's not," Ma responded. "I am your mother, and you should have the chance to do what other girls your age would normally be doing. I know you have had a lot on your plate, and for that, I am sorry."

She boggled my mind. I felt my body grow hotter.

With a tear in her eye, she said," I love you, Charlotte."

I tensed up. I could feel my jaw clench. I did love Ma. She was my mother, after all. I just wasn't sure if she truly loved me.

"I love you, too," I replied.

"Now, why don't you make some of those blueberry muffins you love to bake," she said with a warm smile.

I was left speechless. I never imagined that Ma would ever take ownership of how things have been. I certainly never expected her to say sorry. Despite her not addressing the abuse directly, I supposed that it was a start. Still, I was left feeling perplexed.

I pulled out the blueberries and the rest of the ingredients. I thought about how Ma's moods were unpredictable. One day she was okay, but the next she would be irritable and easy to anger. Before too long, the rich aroma of cinnamon and warm blueberries filled the house.

Ma offered me a cup of coffee. It was something she rarely did because she was usually stingy with her coffee. I gladly accepted it.

"What are the girls studying in school today?" Ma asked.

"Sadie is learning fractions and Anna is learning basic addition," I replied.

"Why don't ya'll take the day off," Ma said. "After all, you didn't take any time off for Christmas this year."

She was right. In a traditional school, we had two weeks of winter break every year. But, this year, Ma had been in such a bad mood that I did whatever I could to keep the girls and myself busy.

Christmas itself wasn't bad. However, it wasn't great either. We didn't do any of our typical family traditions. Usually, Ma would have us help her string popcorn to hang on the tree. And we would bake an enormous amount of homemade Christmas cookies. We girls would decorate them with icing, but we skipped all that this past Christmas.

Ma had spent most of Christmas day in her room. She was extremely depressed and any smile she had flashed us seemed to be forced. I often wondered why us girls weren't enough to make her happy, especially on Christmas. I found myself doing whatever I could to try to make Ma happy anymore. However, it seemed that she missed Daddy too much.

"Sure," I replied to Ma. "The girls would probably be happy to have a break, anyway."

We sat there in silence for a while, just sipping our coffee until the oven beeped, letting me know the muffins were done. I had tried to think of a conversation to start with Ma but I just didn't know how to talk to her anymore.

The girls must have heard the timer themselves because they came rushing into the kitchen to see what had been baking.

"Blueberry muffins!" Anna exclaimed.

"It's been so long since you made some," Sadie said with a smile.

"Okay, girls. They're ready, but we have to let them cool first," I warned them. "Who wants some milk?"

"Me!" they said in unison. They helped me get their cups. They were usually eager to help me. I poured their milk, and as I was placing their cups at the table, Ma gently grabbed my wrist.

"Charlotte, thank you for helping look after the girls. You know they look up to you, right?" she told me. She had a tired but sincere look on her face.

"I know, Ma," I said. "I love them very much."

After the muffins cooled, we all had our fair share of overeating them. The girls both had violet stained faces, and Ma giggled at how silly they looked. We took turns telling knock-knock jokes, and our laughter filled the house.

"What's your plans for today, Charlotte?" Ma asked.

"Well, the potatoes have miraculously survived the winter, so I am going to dig some up for supper. I thought potato soup would be great for this chilly day," I said.

"That sounds perfect!" Ma exclaimed. "Why don't I help you in the vegetable garden. The weeds need pulling anyway."

"Sure!" I said happily. Ma never helped me with chores, so I was glad to accept her offer. And I was especially grateful to spend one on one time with her, which was rare these days.

We each got our coats on and headed out to the vegetable garden. Sure enough, it needed to be weeded. I was thankful for Ma's help today.

As I worked to pull up potatoes, Ma worked to pull up the weeds. Then Ma began singing a song that Grandma used to sing when I was little- "Que Sera". As Ma sang, I chimed in on the chorus.

We continued working and singing. Wind blew and the leaves rustled. I soaked up the scent of fresh earth in my hands. It felt cold and damp. Before I knew it, we were done. Ma had pulled the weeds, and I had a basket full of potatoes. It had been a lovely morning. And, for once, I thought that things would get better.

Before Daddy died, Ma and Daddy did most of the chores. Any chores that I did have, Ma happily helped with. She made a wonderful housewife. But since he died, I took care of the house mostly on my own as Ma couldn't be bothered with it.

We spent the day all watching Disney movies. Sleeping Beauty was Ma's favorite. She said that I was her fairy godmother, here to help her. I thought how wrong that scenario was. I shouldn't be Ma's fairy godmother. But I appreciated the sentiment and her acknowledging how much I helped her. The girls enjoyed Ma's company and were beaming with happiness.

We also enjoyed creating art. Ma did a watercolor painting of a tabby cat that she said used to be a childhood pet. It had been years since I had seen Ma create art, but it was as if she had never stopped. Her painting was gorgeous.

Ma is the one that got me into art. She is the reason that I paint or draw when I am feeling intense emotions. I use it as a way to escape this world, now. Ma said that art was good for the soul and a great coping mechanism.

We ate creamy potato soup for supper. It smelled like coziness inside of a single bowl. Ma had helped me peel the potatoes, which was surprising. I loved the sound of the peeler slicing against the potato. She even helped me clean up afterward and gave the girls their bath. After the girls all had their baths, she put them to bed. We both gave the girls their goodnight kisses and hugs. And then I headed to bed. It was a wonderful day, and I hoped that tomorrow would be just as good.

I don't think I was asleep long when I felt something cold tug at my ankle. I woke up, startled. I turned on my lamp and found the room empty. Perhaps it was just a dream. I pulled my blankets in tighter and shut my eyes. Then, I heard Sadie's music box. I reluctantly got out of bed. The air felt freezing. Nonetheless, I needed to tell Sadie to get back into bed.

I made my way to the hall with a candle, and once at their bedroom door, I saw a dark, shadowy figure lingering over Sadie. He stood about 7 feet tall and wore a black hooded cloak. He turned to me and smiled. His smile was that of crooked, stained teeth that practically glowed yellow in the darkness.

He smelled of rotting meat and embers. He had long hands- longer than natural. His nails looked dirty, like he had clawed his way out of the ground.

"Why hello, Charlotte," he said in a malevolent voice that was smooth and low.

I screamed.

Ma came rushing in. I turned to her and said, "Ma!" But when I turned back to point at him, the man was no longer there, and the music box was no longer playing.

"What is it, Charlotte?" she said worriedly. "And what is that smell?"

"Ma, there was a man there. He was *right there* by Sadies bed," I said, half thinking I was crazy.

Anna and Sadie woke up. Anna looked at us with tired eyes. Sadie has a frightened look on her face with her lips pierced together and her eyes wide. They asked us what's going on.

"Charlotte, there is nobody there. And you have woken the girls," she said with a sneer.

"But I am sure I saw somebody," I pleaded. I began to cry, and my hands were trembling. My heart was seemingly pounding out of my chest.

"Just go back to bed. I will get the girls back to sleep," she replied.

"But Ma, there was a man right there. And Sadie's music box was playing," I cried.

"Charlotte, you're scaring the girls. There is nobody here. Go to my room," she said with her eyes flicking upward.

By this point, both the girls looked scared and Anna began to cry. So, I left the room so Ma could put them back to bed.

I went into Ma's room and sat on the edge of the bed. I was angry that Ma didn't believe me. I know what I saw and the one person that is supposed to help me thinks I am delusional. Ma came in a little bit later with some warm chamomile tea.

"Drink this," she said. "It will help you calm down."

"Ma, I know what I saw," I said.

"Are you sure you didn't dream it?" Ma said.

"No! I was fully awake!" I exclaimed.

25

"Calm down, Charlotte," Ma said. "There has to be some sort of explanation."

I slowly sipped the tea while sitting at the foot of Ma's bed. Ma surely thought I was crazy. Maybe I was. But what I saw and heard seemed so real. Was stress really getting to me?

Ma gently rubbed my back. I tensed up as I was not used to such affection.

"I am glad you are calm now," Ma said. "Do you want to sleep in here? We can make you a pallet on the floor."

I considered it, but then I declined. "No, Ma," I said. "I am fine." I didn't want to sleep in there because I was furious that Ma didn't believe me. Also, Ma had been so distant that it would just be awkward to sleep in her room.

"Okay, Charlotte," Ma said. "If you need me, come wake me up."

"Goodnight, Ma," I told her.

"Goodnight," she replied.

I hesitantly went back to bed, except I couldn't fall asleep. So, I decided to pray. I was praying for God to protect our house and to protect my family. Then, I decided to dive into the family Bible a little more. I was in awe of the symbols on the pages. I decided I would go to the library and see if I could decipher any of the Latin written in the book. As I was sitting in bed, about to blow out my candle, I saw a shadow beneath my door.

"Ma, is that you?" I called out.

My doorknob jiggled, and I yelled louder.

"Ma?!" I cried.

I nearly jumped out of my skin when Ma opened the door.

"What is it, Charlotte?" Ma asked. "And why are you digging in the family Bible again?

"Ma, there was something at my door!" I cried.

"There is nothing there," she said. "Are you sure you don't want to sleep in my room?"

Yes, I do!" I said.

I grabbed my blankets and pillows and made a pallet on Ma's bedroom floor. I made sure I was as close to her bed as possible. There was no way I would be able to sleep alone in my room tonight.

"Why were you in the family Bible again?" Ma asked.

"I was just trying to figure out our family's past," I said sincerely.

"Charlotte, there is nothing to figure out," Ma said with a sigh. "Those days are long gone. You've worked up this giant mystery in your head, and you've freaked yourself out."

"Okay, Ma," I responded flatly.

"Charlotte, I want you to stop meddling in those things," Ma said.

"I will, Ma," I lied.

I felt awful for lying, yet again. However, I had heard and seen enough tonight to know that something was wrong. Our house was haunted. Sadie saw people in her room and now I saw someone, too. Plus, Anna thought someone pushed her off the balcony.

We laid there in silence and the air felt thick. Despite having Ma just a few feet over, I still felt scared and couldn't sleep. Every shadow drawn on Ma's wall in the moonlight gave me chills. I didn't sleep well that night.

Chapter 5

I woke up in a cold sweat. My hair was disheveled and my shirt was soaked. It felt like someone was sitting on my chest. I had the dream again. Well, the nightmare. I had been having the same nightmare for a few weeks. I had seen a bloody hand slap against my window in the dark of the night. It felt so real, and my heart was racing. But now the morning sun shone through Ma's window, so I knew it was just a dream.

I slowly got up off the floor. My head was throbbing, and I was exhausted. I made my way to the kitchen and found Ma drinking her morning coffee and reading the paper. It was odd that Ma was up before me again.

"Ma, I keep having a dream about a bloody hand being at my window," I reluctantly told her. I didn't want to tell her as she didn't believe me last night and I didn't know what she'd say. But I had to tell someone as the nightmare was causing me to lose sleep at this point.

She looked up from her paper and flatly said, "It's a warning that you are going to be caught red-handed. You should be careful what you do and try to hide." Then she went back to her paper.

Ma was always a little superstitious. She believed that everything had a meaning. I just rolled my eyes because I knew that a dream is just a collection of our most creative thoughts strewn together at random.

"Charlotte, make sure you weed the flower garden today. The flowers will never come in this spring if weeds have taken over the garden. And it's supposed to be a sunny day today." Ma directed me.

"Of course. It's been a while since I have pulled the weeds. I'll get to it right away." I responded.

I got dressed and made my way to the garden shed. On the way, I saw Sarah, our closest neighbor, pushing her bike down the road. She always rode her bike to go into town for church services on Sunday.

"Hi, Charlotte!" she said.

"Hi, Miss Sarah! Are you on the way to church?" I replied.

She pulled her bike over by our gate. "Yes, I am. It's a beautiful morning. Enjoying the outdoors today?" she asked.

"Yes, ma'am. I am fixing to tend to the garden and pull the weeds. I am thinking about going for a walk in the forest later to look for mushrooms. There should be some good ones since it has been damp and warmer than usual lately." I told her.

"That's good. Get you some fresh air today. You need to get some time for yourself. How's your Mama doing? I ain't seen her in a few weeks, and I usually run into her in town." she inquired.

"Uh, Ma's been good. She just had her 30th birthday. But she's been a little stressed." I wanted to tell her that Ma had been hiding out in her room all day every day for the past few months, but if word got back to Ma, she'd probably kill me for running my mouth.

"Well, she's got three kids, and with it being around the anniversary of your daddy passing, I am sure she has lots to be stressed about. But I bet she sure is glad to have your helping hand around here." She smiled at me. Sarah's eyes were a soothing blue color, and when she smiled, it was like her eyes were smiling. "And you know if you ever need anything, you can come on by my house. We may not live that close, but we share the same forest, and we are the closest neighbors."

"Yes, ma'am. Thank you, Miss Sarah," I told her.

"Now I'll see you later, Charlotte. Remember to pull the weeds out by the root, or they'll just grow back stronger than ever," she reminded me.

"I got it, Miss Sarah. I'll see you later." I told her.

Miss Sarah and Ma had known each other since they were small children. They used to be inseparable before Daddy died. Now, Ma never made time for her friends.

I got the shovel from the shed and started tending to the garden. These damn roots were in there, alright. I didn't mind weeding the garden normally but I had let these weeds grow way too much. I was surely going to have blisters on my hands by the end of it.

Little by little, I made progress in the garden until I finally finished. Now, it was just a bare garden in the winter. No flowers. No weeds. Just bare. I couldn't wait till spring. When the garden was in full bloom, we had roses, daffodils, violets, and many other colorful flowers. It attracted butterflies and bumblebees. During warmer months, I liked reading on the garden bench while the flowers' fragrance filled my nose.

This winter has been particularly harsh. We hadn't seen much snow, but the cold had made its presence known. Luckily, today was a mild and balmy 50's day, and most of the week was supposed to be just as great. Which meant I would adventure off into the woods. The forest not only brought back good memories of Ma, but it was also a place where I could clear my head and just be me. I craved adventure, and in this small town, the forest was about the only experience that I could get.

I went back inside to wash up before I headed into the forest.

"I want to go with you!" Sadie whined.

Ma, still in the kitchen, told her, "Them woods are dangerous. You know I don't like you kids wandering in them."

"But, Ma! Charlotte gets to go! That's not fair!" She insisted.

"Sadie, Charlotte has been in them woods since she was a little girl. She knows her way, and she is old enough to take care of herself. You haven't been in them woods like her, and she don't need any distractions while she's out there."

"Ma, what's so dangerous about the woods? We've been in there many times, and you used to take me to pick wildflowers in the clearing all the time. Nothing ever happened aside from seeing a common snake occasionally. I can take Sadie with me," I tried to convince her.

"Charlotte, I said no. I have my reasons, and it's not for you to worry about. I don't want you gone any more than an hour, and if you-" Ma started.

"I know. If I see anything odd, I need to come home right away," I finished

Ma's sentence.

"Exactly. So take a watch and be back in one hour. Then you can start getting supper ready. And don't go to the clearing. Remember to pick the big mushrooms only, so the little ones have time to grow," Ma reminded me.

Ma was all about leaving things that were still growing in their place. I never really understood it, but that's what she always taught me ever since I was a small child. Maybe she felt like they needed to live their lives, no matter how short they were.

I grabbed my basket and headed out to the woods.

I loved walking in the forest. It smelled of trees and moss. Even with the trees bare, it was magical to look up at the sky with the branches sprawling outward every which way. Birds sang- at least the ones that hadn't flown south for the winter. Squirrels were particularly active today.

I found a few mushrooms, but I knew that I would find more if I went to the forest clearing. I am not sure what Ma was so worried about. We visited that clearing at least weekly when I was younger. Besides, it would be nice to relive old memories through the wildflowers that were indeed gone until spring. So I set forth toward the clearing.

Once I reached the clearing, I took a deep breath. Winter had definitely come and taken all the colorful wildflowers with it. But that was okay. I immediately spotted a patch of large mushrooms that would be perfect for dinner. I could make mushroom stew.

I bent down to pick the mushrooms, and I heard a low growl behind me. I slowly turned to face a large grey wolf. Well, it was large but looked malnourished. I could see its ribs. I slowly backed away, making sure not to make direct eye contact. Even then, I could see it baring its large teeth. I was trembling and felt my heart beating in my throat. The wolf seemed to match my every step. Suddenly the wolf lunged forward with all its energy. "I am going to die," I thought.

I tripped and fell onto my back. My head thud against the ground. I closed my eyes as I braced for the jaws of the beast. But nothing happened. I slowly opened my eyes and turned around. The wolf had caught a squirrel. I quietly got up and made my way back to the forest. Once I reached the woodline, I ran as fast as I could to get home. Not once did I look around.

I tripped over a tree root and smacked the ground hard. The wind was knocked out of me and, for a second, I struggled to catch my breath. But I got back up as fast as I fell. I ran along the stream until I made it to our backyard. I still refused to look back in case the wolf had followed me. I ran so fast that the world around me was a blur.

When I made it to the door, I rushed inside and slammed the door shut. I was out of breath, but I was finally safe. My head was throbbing, and I felt a little banged up. Grass stains spotted my clothes. Why would a wolf be this close to people? It was sporadic to see one. Even the town's huntsmen rarely saw a wolf in these woods.

Ma asked, "What is wrong?"

I told her, breathlessly, "I- I saw a grey wolf."

"You went to the clearing, didn't you, Charlotte? God damn it. I told you not to go into the clearing." Ma scorned me.

Tears began to swell up in my eyes. "But Ma, I just wanted to pick some mushrooms, and nothing bad has ever happened there." I pleaded. Surely, she would understand since we used to always go to the clearing.

"Charlotte, that clearing is not the same. The presence of a wolf there is a warning. It is not safe," she said.

"But, we always used to go to the clearing!" I exclaimed.

SMACK.

Ma's hand met my face.

"That's the end of it!" Ma yelled. Her face was red and her brows were pushed together.

My face stung as tears rolled down my cheeks. My right cheek felt hot and was indeed red from Ma's hand. I just didn't understand. Why was Ma more superstitious now than ever? She had been extra superstitious the last couple of months. Why was there a wolf in the clearing? Why was I allowed to walk through the forest as long as I stayed away from the clearing? We hadn't visited the clearing since Daddy died. None of it made any sense. And I just had the nagging feeling that something was wrong.

Nonetheless, I had to straighten myself up. I went to the bathroom to splash water on my face. My cheek indeed flushed with pinkness. But there was no place in this house for sulking, and I had dinner to make. Unfortunately, though, the mushroom stew was canceled since I managed to drop the few I had picked. My basket even got wrecked from tripping in the woods.

I ended up making beef stew instead. It was one of my favorite meals, and I insisted on having something I liked for dinner. Ma would order the girls a pizza. I chopped the carrots and potatoes and onions. The sound of the chopping soothed me. The onions made my eyes sting. I placed them in the pot with the stew meat and seasonings. And now it just had to simmer for a while. I stood there for a bit while I watched the stew steam rise. Cooking always relaxed me.

I rubbed some lavender oil on my temples for my headache and decided to lay down on my bed for a while. But I couldn't get the image of the wolf out of my head. Tennessee didn't have wolves until the government decided to introduce them into the ecosystem after a large deer increase. Many of the wolves died off after the deer population was under control. So that's why it was so rare to see one. And they usually stayed so deep in the woods that even local scientists had a hard time tracking them.

I didn't know what else to do, aside from drawing the wolf. So I pulled out my drawing paper and my charcoals and graphite pencils. I was so focused on carefully shading my wolf that Sadie nearly made my heart stop when she started talking.

"What ya doing, Charlotte?" Sadie asked as she peered over my shoulder. "Oh, wow. Did you see a wolf today?"

"Yes, I did," I said, startled. "That is why you girls aren't allowed to come into the woods with me. And you must never wander in there yourself, okay?"

"Okay," Sadie said. "But why was there a wolf in the woods so close to town?"

"I am not sure, Sadie," I said. "Don't worry about it. It just startled me and got a squirrel."

"Can I draw with you?" Sadie asked.

"Of course," I said. "What do you want to draw?"

"I am going to draw an elephant!" she exclaimed.

We sat on my bed for a while, just drawing until dinner was ready. I made Ma a bowl of stew, but she said she wasn't hungry. I wasn't too hungry myself as my head was still hurting, but there was no way I was passing up on stew. I was merrily eating my bowl of stew when I bit down on something so hard that it made my head ring. It appeared to be a tooth. I almost threw up. It looked like a wolf's tooth.

I just had to show Ma. I ran into her room, and I showed her the tooth. She may be in a cynical mood but I just had to show her. Maybe then she would believe the strange things that have been happening around the house. And, surely, she could make sense of it.

"Charlotte, you are hysterical," Ma said. "Calm down. There is no way that is a wolf's tooth. That is just a bone fragment, and it's completely natural, though not desirable, for there to occasionally be pieces of bone in the meat."

"But Ma," I insisted. "It looks just like the teeth of that wolf that I saw today."

"You are just shaken up," she said. "Is your head still hurting?"

"Yes, it is," I replied. Though, I wasn't sure why she cared. She had smacked me earlier and didn't seem to care when she hurt me.

"Take some medicine from the medicine cabinet and try to get some rest," she responded.

So, taking some headache medicine is what I did. After about 30 minutes, my head was no longer throbbing, and I was finally able to relax.

Chapter 6

I made Ma's coffee as usual but then realized she had left a note about going into town for cigarettes on the fridge. She was just going to the corner store, so she'd be back soon. I wasn't supposed to drink her coffee, but I figured why not since I had already made it.

I sat down at the table and read the paper. News in Billington was slow. It was mostly boring stuff about the inauguration of the town elected officials and the harsh winter. We were expecting another winter storm soon. I stumbled upon one article of particular interest. A group of young boys claimed they had spotted a grey wolf, but authorities believed it to be a possible hoax. I shivered and quickly turned to the comic strips.

After I read the comic strips, I rinsed out my empty coffee mug. Then, the phone rang. It was Aunt Cindy calling. I told her about the wolf.

"Charlotte, I need to speak to your mom," she said in seriousness.

"Ma is out right now," I told her. "She should be back soon, though, I said.

"Listen, Charlotte," Aunt Cindy continued. "Mind your momma and do not visit the clearing any more."

"But why?" I asked. "Why can't we go to the clearing?"

"I love you," Aunt Cindy said. "BUt that is for your momma to discuss with you. Anyway, I'm going to head off here. Tell your mom to call me."

"Okay, Aunt Cindy. I love you, too," I said before hanging up the phone.

I was left even more confused. I wanted answers but kept coming up empty-handed. It was best I didn't push too hard, though.

Today, I was determined to do something creative. So I pulled out my watercolor kit. It was a kit that Daddy had gotten from the local art store shortly before he passed away. My kit contained lots of brushes and watercolors of every color you could imagine.

I had been watercolor painting for as long as I could remember. I often paint watercolors in my scrapbook. I was pretty good at it now. Ma had taught me years ago how to use watercolor. She taught me everything I knew about art. She was a fantastic artist herself, even though she hadn't dabbled in art much since Sadie was born. She always said that she didn't have enough time.

It made me sad that Ma didn't paint or draw as much as she used to. We used to set up easels outside and paint the scenery together. Ma would jokingly paint my face and we would laugh and have a great time.

I got my paper ready and picked my favorite brushes. I had my cup full of water and a paper towel. I was going to paint something beautiful. Maybe I would paint the clearing in the woods with wildflowers and the woodline full of greenery and woodland animals. I couldn't wait until spring. The flowers would be in full bloom. Spring always reminded me of good times with Ma. And, maybe, this spring Ma would be willing to collect wildflowers again.

I began painting. Stroke by stroke, I painted what I could remember of the clearing during the most beautiful time of year. I painted violets and dandelions. I painted trees that were green and full of leaves. My thoughts drifted, and once again, I was in the middle of the field picking wildflowers with Ma. We were laughing and having a fabulous time. Each wildflower tickled my senses. Ma held my hands as we twirled around and around. Then I felt cold hands gently around my throat.

I snapped out of my daydream, startled. I put my hands to my throat, but I was okay. I looked down at my painting. I had painted something out of a nightmare. It was a dark figure that was reminiscent of *The Scream* with a large gaping mouth. It had hollow eyes staring back at me.

I quickly pushed the painting away as it gave me chills. What has even happened? One minute I had been painting flowers and then... This? For some reason, I felt scared. My heart was racing, and my palms were sweaty. What was happening to me? Maybe I was just too stressed out.

I put up my art kit and decided to write some poetry instead. My poetry notebook was my sanctuary. Poetry allowed me to write both my best and worst thoughts without worrying about Ma reading them. If she read it, I could always just say it was for the sake of poetry, which she would respect. So I began to write.

Into the night, I go.
My troubles melt away.
Into the night, I go.
Into the black and grey.

Tears welled up in my eyes. I still don't know how my life has become what it has. I was once full of joy and happiness. I felt loved. Now, I feel empty inside and perpetually alone. I am voiceless in a world of chaos and noise. And I just want silence and peace. Is that too much to ask for? I was still distraught over the incidents with the shadow man and the wolf. They had shaken me to my core. I want to tell somebody. I could tell Sarah, but since she is Ma's friend I am not sure how she would handle it. And I didn't want her telling Ma.

I gather myself and check on the girls. They're playing with Barbies and ask if I want to join them in their fashion show. Of course, I did, so I sat down with them. We played for a while. We dressed up Barbies in their best outfits and did the best we could with their knotted hair. We laugh, and I play along, giving each of their fashion choices a score out of 10. It reminded me of when Ma used to play Barbies with me as a young child. Daddy would just watch us and giggle to himself.

After playing with Barbies for a while, we decided to start a 100 piece puzzle. I never really understood the point of puzzles. Unless you were using puzzle glue to keep the puzzle together, what was the purpose of creating something that you would just destroy right after? Nonetheless, the girls enjoyed doing them, and I, frankly, had nothing better to do. Besides, they say puzzles are excellent for your brain anyway. So piece by piece, we built the puzzle.

I thought about how our lives are like puzzles. Each moment is a piece of the puzzle that shapes us into who we are. Who, exactly, was I anymore?

After we finished the puzzle, Sadie decided that she was hungry.

"Well, let's go see what we have," I tell her.

"I want pizza!" she exclaims.

We have some leftover pizza from the night before, so I give her a couple of slices. And she accepts them happily. I make Anna and myself a peanut butter and jelly sandwiches. I spread the creamy peanut butter on Anna's and the crunchy peanut butter on mine. I had always preferred crunchy peanut butter. We happily eat our lunch, and then I ask what the girls want to do next.

"I want to watch a movie," Sadie said.

"Good idea! Let's watch *Snow White*," Anna replied.

We decide that we will watch *Snow White and the Seven Dwarfs* for what feels like the 50th time. It was Anna's turn to choose the movie, anyway. So I put the VHS into the player, and we get all settled. We sang along, "Hi-hoooo." And we laughed at Dopey. We always got a kick out of him no matter how many times we watched the movie.

Ma passes through the living room to head to the kitchen. I can't help but feel nervous and a little scared around her now. She never took things as far as she had the last few days. I was feeling battered. I wanted to retreat to my room, but I couldn't stay in there all day as I had to watch the girls. Ma stops in the living room on her way back through.

"Did you all eat lunch?" she asked.

"Yes. Anna and I had peanut butter and jelly sandwiches, and Sadie had leftover pizza." I tell her.

"Leftover pizza?! Charlotte, that pizza has been out all damn night." She says. Although, I had cleaned the kitchen, I thought the pizza would be fine in its box.

"But we always eat leftover pizza, and it was covered in the box," I say.

"The cockroaches come out at night, and they can get inside the box, Charlotte. You fed your sister cockroach pizza!" She yells.

Ma goes back to the kitchen. I feel like I am going to have a panic attack. My chest feels tight, and my hands are trembling. She comes back from the kitchen with a slice of pizza.

"Eat it. If it's good enough for your sister, it's good enough for you." She

38

orders me.

"But Ma, I didn't know cockroaches could still get to the pizza. I don't want to eat it if roaches have been on it," I plead.

"Charlotte, you will eat this pizza, or I will beat your ass," she says.

After all the times she has slapped me lately, I know that Ma isn't bluffing. I have no idea what she will do if I don't obey her, so I reluctantly take the pizza and eat it bite by bite as I hold back tears. How was I supposed to know that a pizza box wasn't sufficient storage? Again, if Ma had been mothering her children, I wouldn't be in this situation. I tell myself not to let my emotions get the best of me. If I open my mouth, then it will be a lot worse than eating cockroach pizza.

After I eat the pizza, she simply says, "Don't let it happen again." Then she retreats to her room.

I finally let tears fall down my face. I want to be angry at Sadie, but I can't. It's not her fault that I have to look after her and Anna. It's not her fault at all. And it wouldn't be fair for me to take my anger and hurt out on her. That's what Ma was good at doing, and I had to be better than that.

Sadie says to me, "I'm sorry, Charlotte."

"Sadie, it's not your fault. You have nothing to be sorry about," I tell her.

Then, I felt awful for wanting to be mad at her. The girls were consoling me so much lately, and it wasn't fair that they had to worry about me. I was the one supposed to be worried about them. I had to do better. I had to avoid conflict with Ma as much as humanly possible. And I needed to gather some common sense that I had lacked lately. If I got one of the girls hurt or something, I wouldn't be able to forgive myself.

"But Charlotte. Are you okay?" Sadie asked.

"Yeah, Charlotte. Ma has been mad at you a lot," Anna chimed in.

"Girls, I am okay," I reassured them. "Don't you worry about me."

We finished watching Cinderella. Regardless if I gave a single thought to boys or not, I kind of wished a prince would come to rescue me. I don't even need to live in a fancy castle. I just need to get away from this house. I did not feel safe here anymore. And I felt like I was going crazy. I mean, the painting and the hair loss was just the tip of the iceberg. But how was I supposed to stay sane? Ever since her birthday, Ma was ready to rip me a new one nearly every day, it seemed.

Now, I was just feeling furious. So, I decided to walk into town for our mail so that I could calm down. Ma would just have to tend to the girls. We had a post office box in town since Ma didn't trust the mailman to drop the mail in our mailbox ever since winter arrived. I grabbed a jacket, and I stormed out of the house. I walked very briskly to the post office and the whole time I thought of the painting. It frightened me. By the time I got there, I was out of breath as it's a two and a half-mile walk. But, finally, I felt like my head was clear.

The post office was tiny. There were only about ten post office boxes. The postmaster gave me a wave.

"Nice to see you, Charlotte," said Mr. Brinks.

"Nice to see you, too, Mr. Brinks," I said.

I grabbed the mail and headed back home. On the way back home, I took a walk much slower. I kind of regretted not bringing my bike as I was tired. I needed the exercise, though, and it had calmed me down. I just reminded myself that things must get better. I would do better and try to be more careful with the girls. And I would do whatever it took not to make Ma mad anymore. "You have to do this," I thought to myself.

Then, I heard a wolf howling in the distance. I picked up pace until I was practically running. Finally, I made it home, without incident.

When I walked through the door, Ma was in the living room.

"Where have you been?" she asked.

"I went to the Post Office," I replied quickly.

"Why didn't you tell me that you headed to the post office? You can't just leave without saying anything," Ma said. "You just left the girls in the living room by themselves."

"Yes, ma'am," I replied. I didn't want to say a single thing that could make Ma furious.

I gave her the mail and then she left to go back to her room. For the rest of the day, I felt unsettled and restless. Nothing I did could take my mind off the painting.

Chapter 7

Yesterday's mild weather was gone; it had snowed overnight and was still snowing. It blanketed everything outside. The house looked charming, all covered in snow. Behind the house was a barn owl sitting in a tree, and it looked mystical. The girls and I were so excited to play in the snow. While winter had been harsh, we hadn't seen much snow yet this year.

"Sadie, Anna, go get dressed! Put on your coats, your boots, and your gloves!" I told them.

"Yay! I am going to build a snowman!" Anna said.

"I am going to build a snow fort!" Sadie exclaimed.

I was so relieved to get some snow finally. It wasn't even originally in the forecast. The weatherman said the chances of snow were only 10%. Yet it had snowed inches. I welcomed it. A cold winter without snow is like having no reward for enduring the frost. And it had been a cold winter, indeed.

I put on my winter coat even though it was a little too small. The sleeves came up a couple of inches above my wrists. Ma hadn't gotten around to buying us new coats this year. But it wasn't anything that a pair of gloves couldn't fix. I must have had a growth spurt. I was about as tall as Ma now. I slipped my feet into my boots and topped it all off with my favorite winter hat. My long black hair flowed underneath. I left it down for extra warmth.

We went outside, and I found an old rectangular cooler to help Sadie build her fort. We began laying "snow bricks." Daddy had once taught me how to build a snow fort. The memories with him warmed my heart. I missed him so much.

"Charlotte, why doesn't Ma come outside with us?" Sadie asked.

I thought about what to say for a second. Ma hadn't come out of her bedroom often, much less come outside with us. "I think she just wants to be warm inside," I told her. It wasn't exactly a lie. Ma had never been fond of winter. She always loved the warmer months. But, still, there was once a time that she'd never pass up being outside with her kids.

"But she used to come outside all the time. I thought she loved the outdoors," Sadie insisted. There was a gleam in Sadie's eye.

"I don't know, Sadie. Maybe you should ask Ma this," I said, slightly annoyed. I let out a sigh and rolled my eyes.

"You know Ma has a short temper. She gets mad at the littlest things. She would probably get mad at me just for asking," she said, throwing her hands in the air.

"Well, then maybe we ought not to worry about it and just let her be'" I told Sadie.

We had built the lower walls of the fort, so I began working my way upward. I finished the wall then found a bunch of branches to put on top of the roof. The fort was just big enough to sit inside, and it was mighty fine. Daddy would have been proud. Anna came over to examine it.

"Wow! This fort is amazing! Can we keep it forever?" she asked.

"We can keep it until it melts," I told her.

"Awesome!" she exclaimed.

We played inside the fort for what felt like hours. I pretended to have a tea party with the girls. We had snowball fights, played house, and built snowmen guards. It was a fantastic snow day. And I was happy for the new memories that I made with the girls.

"Let's head inside, kiddos. I am freezing," I told the girls while shivering.

The girls immediately met me with resistance.

"But we want to play longer," Anna whined. Her bottom lip stuck out in a pout.

I looked at her sympathetically. The snow is magical when you are little. I remembered playing with Ma and Daddy in the snow before the girls were born. I always thought snow made everything seem like a wonderland. Daddy used to say that snow was a gift from the Gods. "Okay, if you come in without any fuss, I'll make us all some hot chocolate," I promised her.

"Okay!" they both yelled in unison, running inside.

I am pretty sure my fingers were about to fall off. Even with gloves, there was no way to escape the nipping cold outside. I slipped out of my winter gear and put on the fuzziest slippers I owned- unicorn slippers. "Ahh, that feels nice," I told myself. I stood under the vent in my room for a bit until I felt warm again. I sure was glad we had central heating. Ma had central heating installed in the house before I was born. She used to tell me stories about how she used to have to use the old wood stove in the living room to warm the house. I imagined that always gathering firewood was hard. So, thank god for natural gas.

I headed to the kitchen to warm up water in the pot. I pulled out the Swiss Miss hot chocolate packets. I wish I knew how to make homemade hot chocolate, but I didn't, so this would have to do. After the water came to a simmer, I poured the cups and mixed in the hot chocolate. I watched as the powdered chocolate dissolved. Luckily, we had marshmallows, so I topped off each cup with a significant number of them.

"Girls, it's ready!" I hollered, with a smile on my face.

They came running in and took their places at the table. I carefully brought each cup over one by one and warned the girls that it was hot. I told them to be careful. We sat there for a few while the girls tried to count the marshmallows in their cups. Then, suddenly Anna screamed. She had spilled hot chocolate down the front of her shirt.

Ma came rushing in to see what was wrong. She immediately pulled off Anna's shirt and gave her ice to make sure she didn't burn. Anna was crying loudly, and her torso was bright pink. Ma turned to me. Her eyes were wide and her mouth tight.

"You gave them scolding hot chocolate?" she asked me through clenched teeth.

"I told them it was hot and to be careful," I defended myself, despite feeling very guilty.

"Anna is young, and she doesn't know any better! But you do!" she said.

"Give me your hand."

"Why?" I asked fearfully.

"You are going to learn what it feels like! Your stupidity caused her pain so you will feel the same!" she yelled. There was a rage burning in her eyes that I hadn't really seen before. I was terrified.

She grabbed my hand and dragged me over to the stove. She forced my hand inside the pot of the remaining simmering water. I screamed.

"Ma, that hurts!" I cried. I tried to pull away. My heart was racing and I felt like I was going to pass out.

"And you hurt your sister!" she yelled as she pushed my hand deeper into the pot.

I finally yanked it away. I was hurting and furious. So I let the words I had wanted to say slip from my lips. "If YOU took care of YOUR children, this wouldn't have happened. They are not my kids! I don't know how to take care of them!" I yelled with tears streaming down my face.

It was in the moment that Ma was quiet that I knew I had made a big mistake.

SMACK.

She smacked me harder than ever right in the mouth. It stung, and I was stunned. I had fallen to the kitchen floor.

"Get up!" she yelled as she pulled me up by my hair. She pushed me against the wall and wrapped her hands around my throat. I couldn't breathe. I thought Ma really might try to kill me. I tried gasping for air, but I couldn't. I could feel the circulation in my neck being cut off. Surely, my face must have been turning purple.

"You will NEVER talk to me like that, you ungrateful brat!" she yelled. Then she threw me to the floor as she stormed away back to her room.

I laid there for a few minutes crying hysterically. Anna and Sadie came over to me.

"I know it wasn't your fault," Anna said as she wrapped her arms around me. I looked up and saw a single tear make its way down her cheek.

"I love you, Anna. I would never intentionally hurt you." I told her while still sobbing.

"I know," she said. "I love you, too, Charlotte. I am okay."

We all three sat there for a while, embracing one another. Then I wiped the tears from my eyes. I didn't want the girls to think it was their fault. Ma was right. I should have waited until I cooled the hot chocolate before I gave it to the girls. And it was certainly not their fault that Ma just left me to take care of them all day.

I pulled myself up off the floor. My hand was bright pink and a single blister was forming. I took the time to wrap my hand. Thought about how I wanted to die, but I quickly pushed the thought out of my mind as I remembered the girls.

"Let's do some schoolwork," I said.

The girls would usually give me a hard time when it was time to do school work, but neither of them protested. I got their school supplies, and we all sat around the kitchen table. I taught Anna her sight words, and we were working on adding. Sadie was smart for a 7-year-old, so she was working on fractions and persuasive writing. We also looked up elephants, as I had promised Sadie days before.

I enjoyed teaching the girls. Once they sat down to do it, they were terrific students. They each listened to what I said, and they tried their best to succeed at learning. They were quite competitive about getting their schoolwork done despite being at different learning levels.

"It says here that elephants have great memories," Sadie said.

"Awe, look at the baby elephant," Anna cooed.

"It says they stay pregnant for almost 22 months," Sadie said.

We talked about elephants for a while. Then we all spent time writing in our journals. I prompted the girls to write about their snow day. In my journal, I wrote about the incident with Ma. I was still upset. Ma had never gone that far before. And while it wasn't the first time I feared her, it was indeed the first time I feared for my safety. At this point, I wasn't sure how far Ma would go if she got angry at me again. It was as if her eyes were cold at that moment that she was choking me. I had never seen her look like that. And while I was used to getting slapped or even pushed, I would have never expected Ma to do much else.

After writing my thoughts down, I promptly closed my journal and put it away at the top of my closet so that Ma would hopefully never read it. Then, I had the girls share their stories. It was clear they had had a great day.

"Then, we had a tea party inside of the fort!" Anna said.

"And snowmen guards stood outside to protect us from the evil barn owl in the woods," Sadie said. She had quite the imagination. We all laughed.

"Can we use fingerpaint?" Anna asked.

While I hated to clean it up, I still felt terrible for her spilling her hot chocolate on herself so that I couldn't say no.

"Sure," I said. "Just try not to make too much of a mess."

We all finger painted. Sadie painted a portrait of our family. Of course, she even included Daddy. Anna painted a giraffe. And I made a colorful butterfly. I usually didn't finger paint with them, but I didn't have anything better to do. So I let the calm feeling of wet paint beneath my fingers soothe me. It was very relaxing- no wonder the girls liked finger painting so much.

After we finished, I placed our paintings on the fridge using old magnets Ma had collected when she was younger and used to travel. My favorite magnet was the one from Alaska. I wish we could travel. Ma said the mountains in Alaska were the most beautiful sight she had ever seen. She even got to see a grizzly bear while she was there.

I had never even left the state. Ma said that family vacations were too expensive. The best thing we got to do was go to Dollywood every summer. But we hadn't gone since Daddy died. We hadn't even left the town since he died. And there was nothing to do here for kids.

For the rest of the day, we took the time to read and relax. I was thankful because even though the day had started great, I was mentally exhausted from the incident with Ma. Every time she came out of her room the rest of the day, I held my breath, waiting for her to be angry at me again over something. Luckily, the day was without further incident.

Chapter 8

I lie awake in my room. It's cold, so I have extra blankets on the bed, but it nips at my nose so I can't entirely fall asleep. I decided to read *Bag of Bones*. Stephen King's work always took me to a different place. A place, perhaps, more terrifying than reality. That somehow soothed me.

Carefully reading each line at a time, the book consumed me. Almost so consumed that I didn't hear the footsteps in the hall. But, indeed, I did hear them. I thought to myself, "It must be one of the girls." I carefully get out of bed to see who is wandering around the house at this hour.

I peer out into the hall, but I see nobody. Hm. They must've gone back to bed. I crawl back into my bed and continue with the book. But only a few moments later, I hear the footsteps again. So, once again, I get out of bed. There was nobody in the hall, again. I check the girls' room, and they're fast asleep. As I look into Ma's room, where she was also asleep, I hear footsteps behind me. I slowly turn to see a shadow cast upon the wall as if someone walked into my room.

I quietly grabbed a nearby candlestick and made my way back to my room. I hear footsteps as if someone is pacing around my room over and over. My heart is beating louder than I am breathing. I am grasping the candlestick so tightly that my knuckles are white. I look around the corner of my doorway, expecting to come face to face with an intruder. Yet, nobody is there. I let out a deep breath after having held it up until this point.

I decided to check out the living room and the kitchen. Both were empty. Was I so exhausted that I imagined things? Or perhaps the book had gotten the best of me. I settled back in my bed and started to drift off to sleep. Yet the footsteps returned. I could even see a shadow pacing the hallway beneath the crack under my door. This time, I remained in bed until the morning.

"Ma, I heard footsteps in the hall last night, but nobody was there," I told her as I gave her her coffee.

"Charlotte, have you been reading those horror novels in bed again? Of course, you hear things. Those books are terrifying as they're meant to be," she said with a shiver.

"I know, Ma. But I swear they sounded so real. And I even saw a shadow enter my room," I proclaim. I just wanted her to believe me.

"Well, maybe it was just a shadow from the pile of clothes in your room that you haven't put away," she says, giving me a side-eye.

"Ma, it looked like a man. And I saw a shadow under my door," I protested.

"Charlotte, if you went to bed at a decent hour instead of reading those scary stories, you might not scare yourself half to death," she replied.

"Ma, I know what I saw. But okay. I will put away my clothes now," I responded.

I went to my room to tidy up and put my clothes away. As clean as I kept the rest of the house, you would never know it was judging by my room. It was a disaster. Who knows. Maybe that was the shadow I saw.

I put away the clothes. I made my bed. And I tidied up the floor. The floor... On the floor was a dusty footprint. I put my foot next to it, but it was a little bigger than mine. Maybe it was Ma's footprint, but she practically never went into my room. Whose footprint could it be? "Could it be from last night?" I wandered. Chills ran down my spine. Then I felt a hand on my shoulder and nearly jumped out of my skin.

"Charlotte! I can't find my talking Elmo," Sadie said.

"Jesus Christ, Sadie! You nearly gave me a heart attack," I scolded her.

"I am sorry! But can you help me find my talking Elmo?" she asked.

"Sure, kid," I tell her.

We head to the girls' room. The smell of rotting meat is in the room again. I look around, though, and their space is quite tidy as I recently cleaned it.

"What is that smell?" I ask while holding my nose. "Have you or Anne been eating in here?"

48

"No! We know we would get in trouble for eating in our room," Sadie says.

I locate her talking Elmo and then quickly head out of there. I tell Ma about the smell.

"Well, if you just cleaned it, maybe there is a rat stuck in the wall," Ma said.

"A RAT?!" I cry loudly.

"Well, we do live in the woods, and sometimes those things happen. I'll call Bobby here in a bit and have him come take a look."

"Oh. Great," I say accidentally out loud. Bobby has a real hankering for Ma. He lives in town, but he occasionally has helped out Ma with handy work around the house. But Bobby gives me the utter creeps with his potbelly always hanging out of the bottom of his stained t-shirts. And he always looks like he hasn't shaved in a week. Nothing more on his face, nothing less.

"Charlotte, be nice," Ma said with a chuckle. "Bobby is great help. And nobody is trying to take your Daddy's place."

I just sighed audibly and gave my shoulders a shrug.

Later in the day, Bobby comes to inspect. He looks everywhere but comes up empty-handed.

"Well, Luna, there is nothing here. And, frankly, I don't even smell it anymore. Maybe one of the little ladies let one rip in there," he tells Ma.

She laughs at his corny, dumb joke. "See, Charlotte. Nothing to worry about," she assures me.

"Sure," I say and roll my eyes at Bobby.

"Now, now, missy. Why the attitude?" Bobby asked with a grin.

I didn't respond.

"Well, Bobby, while you are here, can you take a look at a small leak we have at our outside spigot?" Ma asked.

"Of course! I'll do anything for the beautiful Luna," Bobby said, winking at her.

I nearly threw up in my mouth. Ma was way too good for someone like Bobby. He always smelled of pits and car oil. And his hair was never kempt. Daddy looked nor smelled nor acted like Bobby in the least. Bobby could never live up to those standards for Ma.

Nonetheless, at least he did help Ma around the house free of charge. As much as I tried to help, there were certain things I just wasn't knowledgeable in. I did know one thing, though. That scent was ferocious.

That was the third time I smelled that scent, and none of the times did I find anything. Maybe it was just a smell that this old house had to it sometimes. But I remembered that in *The Amityville Horror,* they had a rotten smell, and it was a demonic entity. I shuddered. I watched and read far too much horror.

There were too many strange things going on, but I was sure that I was letting my imagination run away from me. Things had been so stressful, and I was just tired. I was tired of always walking on eggshells around Ma. I was tired of regularly taking care of the girls and the house. And I was tired of being tired.

Still, I had to get the girls ready for homeschool. Today, we were studying the planets. Science was the girls' favorite subject. I gathered the materials we needed, and we sat down in the living room.

"Why does Bobby like Ma so much?" Sadie asked.

"I don't know, Sadie," I said.

"Well, he is weird," Sadie said with a scrunched up face.

She sure had that right. Anna was the only one that took a liking to Bobby. She enjoyed his corny jokes. Sadie and I couldn't stand him, though. And since he had been friends with Daddy, we found it extra weird that he had a thing for Ma.

Together, the girls and I made styrofoam planets. We used Ma's encyclopedias to look up fun facts about each world. The girls each giggled when we got to Uranus. I would have been rolling my eyes, but I remembered how funny I thought it was when I was little, too.

We went to their room to hang their planets from the ceiling when we realized that the smell had returned. I immediately called for Ma and Bobby.

"Guys, the smell is back!" I yelled down to the basement. I could hear Ma giggling, and that repulsed me.

They came back upstairs, grinning.

"Well, I sure do smell it now!" Bobby said.

"What can we do about it?" Ma asked, holding her nose.

"I am not sure there is much we can do, Luna," Bobby said. "I don't think it's a rat. Maybe you have a leak. I'll check the attic."

I continued hanging the planets up in the girls' room. It looked like a charming solar system on their ceiling. Bobby was in the attic for a while. He yelled down that all was clear. So we gathered at the foot of the attic.

On his way down from the attic, Bobby seemed to have lost his footing on the ladder, and he fell straight on his back. I couldn't help but snicker. Ma gave me a stern look, and I quickly stopped.

Bobby moaned and struggled to get back up.

"Bobby, are you okay?" she asked sympathetically.

"I'm fine, but I think one of your little ladies grabbed my ankle," he said in an angry voice.

Ma hollered, "My girls might be a handful at times, but they would never do such a thing!"

"Luna, I am just telling you what happened!" Bobby yelled.

It was at that moment I thought Ma might slap him. Nobody yelled at Ma. Her face turned bright pink, and she had a severe look on her face.

"Get out, Bobby. I have had enough of your help today," she said sternly. Her eyes were narrow and her jaw was clenched.

"Come on now, Luna," Bobby said. "I was just telling you that I think one of them grabbed my foot."

"Bobby, I don't care what you think," Ma said. "You have about five seconds to get out, or I'm putting you out."

I was shocked that Ma stuck up for us. Then again, I knew that she didn't have the same hankering for Bobby. I was sure that she just tolerated him and flirted back for a free helping hand. However, what if Bobby did feel somebody grab his ankle? I suddenly thought back to the day that Anna felt someone push her from the balcony. I got chills.

Bobby left, and we handled the smell the best way we knew how to- with a ton of Lysol. We sprayed so much Lysol that we could taste it in the air. Then, Ma had us open the windows to let it air out. Since it was so cold outside, the girls played in my room for the rest of the day. I let them have at it with my art supplies. We hung out for a while, painting and drawing whatever came to our imaginations.

"Ma, thank you for sticking up for us," I said.

"Of course, I will stick up for you, girls," Ma said. "Bobby is a generous man, and I don't think he meant anything by it. I think he just got disoriented."

That night, the smell was still lingering. So, Ma just instructed me to make a pallet on the floor of the living room for the girls to sleep, so they didn't have to endure the scent. I laid out blankets and pillows for them.

"Charlotte, will you watch *X Files* with us?" Sadie asked.

"Certainly! You know I wouldn't miss *X Files* night!" I exclaimed.

I laid with the girls and watched reruns all night long. I kept thinking about Bobby's accusation and decided to sleep with the girls.

Chapter 9

Ma went into town to get groceries. She went every two weeks or so. She instructed me to clean out the fridge and get the kitchen cleaned while she was gone. Cleaning the kitchen meant sanitizing the counters, washing the dishes, cleaning the stove, and cleaning the baseboards and floors. And I had about 30 minutes to do all of it.

I was cleaning out the fridge when Sadie came in. "Anne pinched me!" she cried.

She had a small little blood blister on her arm.

"Anne, come here!" I yelled.

"What?!" she replied when she made it to the kitchen.

"Why did you pinch, Sadie?" I asked. My hands were on my hips.

"Sadie told me I am stupid. So I pinched her," she responded sincerely.

Anne could do many things but knowing how to lie was undoubtedly not one of them.

"Well, go sit on the couch for 15 minutes," I ordered her.

"But that's not fair! She called me stupid," Anne resisted, her face turning pink..

"Yes, and that's not okay. But we don't lay our hands on people regardless of how mad we get," I told her.

"Ma does!" she replied.

I was stunned. Anna wasn't wrong. Ma did put her hands on people as punishment.

"Well, Anna, you aren't Sadie's mother, and you have no right to determine what a fair punishment is. Sit on the couch for 15 minutes. NOW," I replied harshly.

She huffed and puffed and stomped her feet the whole way out of the kitchen.

"Sadie, you can't call your sister stupid. That's not nice. Now, help clean out the fridge," I told her.

"No. I didn't call Anna stupid, and I don't want to help clean out the fridge," she lied.

Sadie liked to tell fibs even though she was terrible at it. She was always lying about something. And she loved getting Anne into trouble. That wasn't the issue, though. I wasn't sure what to do, considering she had blatantly told me that she would not help with the fridge. If it were Ma, there is no way she would have said no.

"You know damn well that Anna doesn't just make things up, " I told her. "You need to help me. I have less than 30 minutes to finish cleaning this kitchen because of you two, and I am not even done with the fridge. Ma will be pissed if she gets back, and I haven't done it."

"I will not help you clean out the fridge. I don't have to. Ma told you to do it," she protested.

"Yes. And Ma also told me to watch you two. But since you can't behave, I have to take care of it. You will help me clean out the fridge, or I will just be sure to tell Ma what happened," I warned her, knowing that Anna would surely tell Ma anyway so I wouldn't have to.

She finally started helping me. We threw out old food and wiped down every shelf of the refrigerator, making sure that it looked as good as new. Then I let her play again. I washed the countertops, mopped the floor, and cleaned the baseboards. It smelled like Murphy Oil Soap. I loved that smell. Just as I was getting ready to clean the stove, I heard the door open and panicked.

"Come get the groceries, Charlotte," Ma said.

I felt a sudden doom. Ma would quickly realize that I hadn't finished the kitchen, and she would be fuming. I promptly went outside to get groceries and hoped that she would overlook that I had yet to clean the stove.

As I was bringing the groceries back in, Ma started yelling.

"Charlotte, I asked you to do one God damned thing while I was gone getting groceries for you girls!" she yelled. "Put the groceries up, and then you're going to finish this mess."

"But Ma, the kids were acting up, so I didn't have time to finish," I tried to defend myself.

She left the room without saying a word, and I was left there puzzled. So, I began putting groceries away. I was bending down to put the lettuce in the fridge's drawer when something suddenly hit me across the back. I cried out in pain. Ma had struck me with the buckle end of a belt.

"I have told you time and time again not to backtalk me!" Ma yelled.

She hit me again. This time the buckle struck my shoulder. I stood up to defend myself, but Ma only hit me again, this time across the back of my legs.

"Stop, Ma! That hurts!" I cried with tears rolling down my face.

However, she didn't stop. She hit me again and again and again until I could no longer stand.

"If you hadn't backtalked me, I would have gone on my way as long as you were ready to finish after putting up the groceries," she said, hitting me in the back again.

I cried aloud.

"Do you understand me now when I say no back-talking?" she asked.

"Yes, ma'am," I replied quickly.

She hit me a few more times. I could feel the buckle striking me every time. My whole back was on fire.

"Now finish the fucking kitchen," she told me. And she left to go to her room.

I sat on the kitchen floor, sobbing. My back and my legs were throbbing. I finally forced myself up to go to the bathroom to rinse my face. I turned my back to the mirror, and I could see blood through my pale yellow t-shirt. Ma had battered my back and legs. Welts and cuts marked my skin. It would take days for this to heal.

I looked in the mirror and saw a lost little girl staring back at me. "How did it come to this?" I asked myself. I couldn't stop the tears, no matter how hard I tried. I felt so lost. So alone. "How can I keep living like this?" I wondered.

After changing my shirt, I went back to the kitchen and cleaned the oven the very best that I could, coughing from the fumes of Easy-Off. That was the thing, you see. Even though it shouldn't have been my responsibility to clean the house, look after the kids, and tend to the garden, I always took pride in everything I did. I made sure that I did everything well. I had made a few mistakes lately, but I still thought I was doing a pretty good job, considering. If only Ma could see it, too.

After I finished cleaning the kitchen, I went to my room and cried for an hour. I just let the tears pour. Then, Ma walked past my room. She stopped at the doorway. I thought I was going to get in trouble again for crying.

"Charlotte, I hate punishing you, but I have told you not to backtalk," Ma said emotionlessly. "When I say to do something, you just say 'Yes, ma'am,' and you do it. Do you understand?"

"Yes, ma'am," I replied through my sobs.

"Now, what is this I heard about Sadie calling Anna stupid?" Ma asked.

"She called Anna stupid, and I made her help me with the fridge," I replied.

"Well, that is not punishment enough," Ma said. "You should have sent her to her room."

Ma always confused me. I was in charge of punishing the girls while she was away or in her room. But I could never seem to get it right.

"Anna pinched her in return," I said, trying to convince her that Sadie got her punishment.

Lord knows she wasn't going to punish Anna.

"Sadie needs to sit in her room for the rest of the day until dinner," Ma said. "And have her write that she will not call her sister stupid 200 times."

Ma loved giving me writing sentences as a punishment when I was little, so I wasn't surprised.

"Okay, Ma," I responded.

I gathered writing materials and called Sadie from the living room.

"Sadie, come here, please," I yelled.

She entered my room and asked what I wanted.

"Ma wants you to stay in your room until dinner," I replied. "Also, you need to write 'I will not call my sister stupid' 200 times."

"But Charlotte! What about Anna?" she asked.

"I don't know, Sadie," I responded. "Ma didn't say anything about Anna."

"Well, did you tell her she pinched me?" she cried.

"Of course I told her," I said. "But Ma didn't seem to think that Anna deserved any more of a punishment than she got already."

"That's not fair!" Sadie whined. SHe had tears in her eyes.

"Well, life isn't fair, Sadie!" I snapped.

I gave her the writing pad and pencil and told her to get to her room.

I felt awful for Sadie. She was right, after all. It indeed wasn't fair. But she was lucky that her punishment wasn't any more than it was after what I had dealt with today. It was more apparent than ever, though, that Anna was Ma's favorite. Sometimes I wondered if Ma hated Sadie and me because we looked like Daddy so much. But I would never know. And I know that Sadie saw that Anna was Ma's favorite. It hurt me knowing that. Ma shouldn't make her 7-year-old resent her younger sister. There was enough friendly competition among siblings for that to occur on its own.

I decided to sit in the girls' room to keep Sadie company. It was bad enough that Ma punished her; I didn't want her to feel alone. Loneliness is a heavy emotion to carry. I needed her to know that I was on her side and would always be there for her.

So I sat there watching her write her sentences one by one. I corrected her when her writing started to get sloppy as I knew Ma would make her redo them all if even just one sentence was unreadable. Eventually, she completed her sentences and turned them into Ma. I heard Ma yelling at her for calling Anna stupid, and Sadie cried. But that was that. At least it was settled.

We sat in the room for some time. I read Sadie *Harry Potter*. Ma didn't like us reading it much because she said it wasn't very Christian. But she refused to forbid us from reading it because she felt it was more important that we had a love for reading. As we were reading the book, Sadie talked about how wonderful it would be for each of us to get letters for Hogwarts. And I couldn't have agreed more. I did feel like Harry sometimes, and I knew that, at that moment, Sadie felt like Harry, too.

Finally, when it was dinner time, I asked Ma if Sadie could come out of her room.

"Yes," Ma said. "But next time you aren't sitting in there with her."

"Yes, ma'am," I responded.

"You baby Sadie and stick up for her too much," Ma said. "She is going to have to learn to deal with the consequences of her actions and that you're not always going to be there to bail her out."

I just stared at Ma speechless. The irony was how she treated Anna, but I certainly couldn't say that to her. And Sadie was honestly a great kid aside from the story-telling. I hate how Ma acted as if she were always acting up. Nobody should think of their small child that way.

"Now, go put on some of those frozen pot pies for dinner," Ma said.

"Yes, ma'am," I responded. And I quickly left her room before I did or said something to get into further trouble.

During dinner and even after, the house was tranquil. Anna had tried to convince Sadie to play with her, but Sadie understandably gave her the silent treatment. So, we ended the day with Sadie quietly hanging out in my room and Anna spending alone time in theirs. I think everybody, except Anna, was on edge. And rightfully so

Chapter 10

It was a gloomy day.

Dark clouds filled the sky, and it was freezing outside. Sadly, there was no snow in the forecast. Nor was there any sunshine.

The girls were antsy and bored. So, we settled on making a blanket fort in the living room. We draped a king-size sheet over the furniture and brought in an army of stuffed animals. The girls grabbed their favorite books for me to read to them. It was an idea that I got from Ma as she used to make blanket forts with us all the time.

We laid in there for quite some time. I read multiple Berenstain Bears books. I read a book of Mother Goose nursery rhymes. We read some of Goosebumps *Welcome to Dead House*. Reading was one of our many ways to escape life. And we often read together.

Still bored, we decided to play with our Lite Brite. We made all kinds of shapes and pictures. We laughed and had a good time. That was until Sadie called Anna stupid again.

"Sadie! You cannot call Anne names and especially not stupid!" I yelled at her.

It was at that moment that Ma came storming into the living room.

"What did I hear about Sadie?" Ma asked seriously.

"Sadie called me stupid again!" Anna quickly said.

"Excuse me? Sadie, go grab a spatula right now," she told her firmly.

Sadie quickly got a spatula, and Ma yanked it from her.

"Turn around," she said.

Ma proceeded to hit Sadie with the spatula over and over again until Sadie said the unthinkable.

"I hate you!" she cried.

Ma immediately slapped her across the face and then dragged her to her room by a fistful of hair. I overheard her telling Sadie not to come out of the room until dinner. I looked at Anna, and she looked mortified. I don't think she meant for Sadie to get beat.

Being the youngest, Anna was mostly safe from Ma's outbursts. She could ultimately get away with murder, and Ma would just brush it off as if she were a baby. I felt terrible for Sadie and felt resentment toward Anna. Whenever the girls acted up, I always tried to take matters into my own hands, so they, especially Sadie, didn't have to deal with Ma's wrath.

I think Anna was learning that Ma would overreact to most things. Anne didn't like seeing us getting physically punished, and it was from that moment that she would probably not tattle-tale again, even if she didn't realize it at the time.

I went to the girls' room to console Sadie.

"It's going to be okay; let me have a look, " I told her as I lifted the back of her shirt. She, too, now had welts and bruises along her back. "Let me get you some ice," I said softly.

I went to the kitchen to get some ice and met Ma instead.

"What are *you* doing?" she asked me with a handful of attitude.

"I am just getting Sadie some ice for her back," I told her wearily.

"Sadie will be just fine. All she did was get a little ass-whoopin' for calling y'all's sister names. Now, go clean up the living room. I have already told you not to continue going after Sadie's rescue," she said.

I quickly left the kitchen to get away from Ma before I found myself in trouble of some kind. I took down the blanket fort and put away the books and stuffed animals. I then sat down on the couch. I wasn't sure what to do with myself. It seemed as though we had watched every one of our Disney movies more than once this winter. I didn't feel like making art. And the house was pretty clean. And I definitely could not console Sadie, or Ma might take her wrath out on me.

I glanced at the coffee table and noticed the family Bible. It had been years since I really looked at it. So, I figured I would flip through it again. There were pictures of family members- many of whom I didn't even know. There were notes by various scriptures. I figured it's the typical family bible.

However, there were weird symbols drawn among some of the pages and some Latin writing. When I got to the end of the bible, there were loose pages of notes written in Latin. One page looked like a recipe with the words "Vitam Aeternam" written across the top. I had no idea what any of it said. That's when I decided to go to the library.

"Ma, I'm going to the library," I told her as she laid in her bed.

"Okay. Hurry back to make dinner," Ma said. "And get me a romance novel. One I haven't read."

I walked into town. It was not as busy as usual. I am assuming it was due to the cold. It was a bummer because I usually enjoyed the bustle of townsfolk walking about the streets. But I still got to enjoy the scent of someone roasting turkey legs over an open fire at a small stand on the corner.

I walked past the chocolate shop, and it smelled amazing. I walked past a toy shop with porcelain dolls in the window. Those things gave me the creeps. I walked past a shop with beautiful Sunday dresses in the window and wished that I could buy the lilac one. Finally, I made it to the library.

Once I walked inside, I found Mrs. Hensworth, the town librarian, for the past forty years.

"Hi, Mrs. Hensworth!" I said excitedly.

"Well, hello, Charlotte! How can I help you today? Are you checking out another romance novel for your mom?" she asked.

"Yes, I am. But I wonder if you have any translation books to help me translate some Latin," I told Mrs. Hensworth.

"Of course, dear! Follow me!" she said enthusiastically.

I followed her into the maze of bookshelves when she handed me a thick book.

"I'll let you be, now," she said. "Come checkout when you're ready."

The book was heavy in my hands and had a brown leather cover. It looked ancient. It smelled ancient, too, but in an enchanting way. I loved the scent of old books. I looked up the words I had found earlier and discovered that they meant "eternal life" or something of that nature. I would be checking out this book. I searched the shelf for any more books that might help me and found one for ancient Latin symbols. Some of the signs reminded me of some of the ones I had seen drawn in the family bible, so I took that with me as well. I made sure to grab Ma a romance novel called *Warriors Woman*, and then I was on my way.

Outside of the library, I ran into Sarah.

"Hi, Charlotte! Coming from the library?" she asked.

"Yes, ma'am. I had to get a book for Ma," I half-lied.

"Well, what're those other books? Latin? Why are you researching Latin?" she asked.

"Oh. Um. I have just been bored and am trying to learn some Latin," I lied to Miss Sarah.

"Oh, okay. You are one of the brightest kids in town," she told me.

I blushed and felt a little bad for lying to her. "Thanks, Miss Sarah," I told her.

"I'll catch you later, Charlotte," she said. " I may stop by on Sunday to bring you guys some of my banana bread. It's delicious, but I made far too much for just myself."

"We would love that! Thank you, Miss Sarah. I'll see you later," I said.

I finished the walk home. Inside my room, I tucked away the Latin books. I don't know why but I had a nagging feeling that Ma wouldn't want me translating the pages in the family Bible. I mean, if she had wanted me to know what the words and symbols intended, she would have told me long ago. Besides, she had made it clear she didn't want me meddling in it.

It was dinner time, so Sadie was once again let out of her room. She kept giving Anna dirty looks, and Anna mostly kept her head down until she apologized.

"I'm sorry, Sadie," she said. "If I had known… I wouldn't have said anything."

"Well, you DID say something because you are a tattle-tale that never gets into trouble," Sadie hissed back.

"I said I am sorry!" Anna cried.

"Sorry for what? Being Ma's favorite?" Sadie snapped.

"That's enough," I said firmly. "In this life, all you have is family. And I'll be damned if us sisters are going to go at each other's throats. We have to stick together, do you understand?"

"Yes, Charlotte," Anna said.

Sadie just looked at me like I was growing a third eye.

"Sadie, your sister couldn't have known that you were going to get into so much trouble," I said. "There is no reason to hold a grudge against her, and she said sorry. Do not forget that she is your *sister*."

"Fine. I'll drop it," Sadie said flatly.

"Now, what do we want to do tonight before bath time?" I asked.

Neither girl answered.

"Fine, we will play go-fish," I said.

And that is precisely what we did. Luckily, neither girl held a grudge for too long. Before I knew it, they were laughing and getting along just fine. Then, Ma came out of the room.

"Sadie, did you apologize to Anna?" she asked.

Anna quickly lied for the first time ever, "Yes, she did." Anna glanced over at me as if to tell me not to spoil her lie.

"That's good," Ma said. "What are you girls playing?"

"Go-Fish!" Anna exclaimed.

"Can you deal me in," Ma asked?

I felt bewildered. Ma never played with us anymore. And after the events of the last couple of days, I wasn't sure why Sadie's eyes lit up so much. I wanted nothing to do with Ma and didn't understand why Sadie did.

I reluctantly dealt Ma into the game. We sat there in the living room, as a family, playing Go-Fish for about an hour. Ma and the girls seemed to be having a great time. It was the first time Ma had smiled in days. Both Anna and Sadie were smiling ear to ear, too. It was an excellent sight to see, but it just felt forced and awkward to me.

I finally sighed a breath of relief when Ma said she had played enough for the night. Surprisingly, she offered to get the girls ready for bed. However,

I was still scorned, so I declined her help. So, as with every night, I bathed them, got them their glasses of water, read their bedtime stories, and tucked them.

I then set off to clean the kitchen. Ma followed shortly after.

"I am glad you didn't baby Sadie today," Ma said.

Without knowing what else to say, I replied, "Yes, ma'am."

"She will learn quickly that there are repercussions for her actions," she replied. "Do you need help with the kitchen?"

I would insist Ma not help me with the kitchen as it would just be awkward. I just wanted her to go away. But I was afraid that she might get mad if I declined her help again, so I reluctantly replied, "Sure."

Ma washed the dishes and cleaned the counters while I swept and mopped the floors. It took me half the time that it usually did cleaning the kitchen.

"This is how a family is supposed to be," I thought to myself.

"Thanks, Ma," I said to her.

"Your welcome, Charlotte," she said. "You girls have had a rough couple of days, so I figured I would pitch in." With that, she headed to her room, and I got ready for bed.

Chapter 11

When I went to bed, I took the family Bible with me. I carefully translated some of the words. The recipe seemed to be more of a spell- one for eternal life. The symbols on the pages turned out to be sigils. Some represented angels; some represented demons. Others were various representations of occultism, according to the book I had borrowed from the library.

None of this made sense. Ma was strictly Christian, and we went to a typical Southern Baptist church in town when we did go to church. Why would there be symbols of the occult in the family Bible? Why was "As above, so below" written in Latin on the back of my great-aunt's photo? I had so many questions, and I was afraid to ask Ma.

My head was spinning, and I decided I needed a break and that it was time for bed. Just as I shut my lamp off, I heard a "thump, thump, thump" against the wall. I waited a few moments, and then I heard another "thump, thump, thump." I got out of bed and decided to investigate the sound. It was coming from Ma's room, and I thought she would surely be asleep by now.

I peered inside her door and heard the thumps again. In the moonlight, I saw Ma dressed in her nightgown facing her wall. Her hair was flowing wildly against her shoulders. She looked paler than usual in the moonlight. She was saying something over and over, but I couldn't hear her. So, I moved closer to her. "Ma, are you okay?" I asked.

"Can't escape. I can't escape. Can't escape," Ma quickly repeated.

Then, "thump, thump, thump," she banged her head hard against the wall in threes. I was startled and wasn't sure what to do. She seemed to be sleepwalking, and I had heard somewhere that you shouldn't wake sleepwalkers. I decided to guide her to her bed carefully. I put one head against her forehead to stop her from banging it against the wall. I put another hand in hers to pull her away. I got her to lay down, and I covered her up. Even in the darkness, I could see that Ma's forehead was pink. I was practically tip-toeing to her door in order not to wake her when she suddenly screamed.

"CANNOT ESCAPE!! CANNOT ESCAPE!!" she yelled.

I rushed by her side, where she was sitting fully erect in her bed. Her eyes were open, but they glossed over and cold. Her pupils were tiny, and something wasn't right. I frantically shook her shoulder. "Ma, I think you're having a nightmare. Ma, wake up. Ma, you have to wake up."

She blinked, and then she looked at me with clarity.

"What's wrong, Charlotte? Why aren't you in bed?" she asked.

"Ma, you- you were having a nightmare, I think," I stuttered.

"Well, I am fine now. Go back to bed," Ma said hoarsely.

"Ma, you were banging your head against the wall, and then you were screaming," I said.

"Charlotte. Go back to bed now," Ma said firmly.

I quickly left her room. I wasn't sure what had just happened, but something was not right. I had never seen Ma sleepwalk. She was a hefty sleeper and hardly budged at night. I shivered and then turned around to go back to bed. Both girls greeted me at the door.

"What's wrong with Ma," Sadie asked.

"She is fine. I think she just had a nightmare," I said, shuddering.

"What did she have a nightmare about?" Anna said, wide-eyed.

"I am not sure. But there is nothing to worry about as Ma is fine now. Now, let's get you two back in bed," I said, guiding them to their room.

After I got the girls back to bed, I was ready for bed myself.

The next morning, I awoke to the smell of cinnamon and syrup filling the house. It smelled so warm and cozy and took me back to happier times. I pulled my blanket over my shoulders as it was still abnormally cold in the house. I made my way to the kitchen, where I found Ma standing over the stove, making french toast.

"Good morning, Charlotte!" Ma exclaimed.

It had been months since Ma made breakfast. And I don't know the last time she told me good morning. It was as if she had slept better than she ever had.

"Good morning, Ma," I said cautiously. "Do you need help?"

"Charlotte, I *do* know my way around the kitchen, ya know. Just set the table for us, and I'll take care of the rest," she said with a smile.

"For us?" I asked myself. Ma indeed wasn't eating breakfast with us. Right? She always ate in her room. Nonetheless, I set the table for the four of us. Ma filled the plates with stacks of french toast and poured tall glasses of orange juice for everyone.

"Go get the girls," Ma said.

"Anna. Sadie. Ma has made breakfast and wants to eat with us," I tell them.

"Ma is eating breakfast with us?" Anna asked with sparkles in her eyes.

"I guess so, kiddo," I said.

We all sat down at the table.

"Let's say a prayer," Ma said. "Anna, why don't you say it."

"God is great. God is good. Let us thank him for our food. Amen," Anna led.

"Amen," we all repeated.

"How did everyone sleep?" Ma asked.

"I slept great!" Sadie said.

"How did *you* sleep?" I asked Ma curiously.

"I slept like a baby!" She exclaimed.

"Ma, you don't remember anything from last night?" I asked.

"What do you mean?" she inquired.

"You had a nightmare!" Anna exclaimed.

"Well, I remember nothin' of the sort," Ma said, smiling gently.

This morning is so odd. Ma must not remember anything about last night, yet she had a bruise on her forehead. And she was in the best mood I have seen her in since... well since Daddy died. Since she was in such a good mood,

I decided to risk it and ask about the family Bible.

"Ma... The family Bible has symbols and Latin written in it. Why?" I asked.

Ma gave me a peculiar look. One that warned me not to ask anything further. But she also looked curious to know why I was asking.

"It's just old family scribblings. Nothing more. Nothing less." Ma said.

"But Ma, how does our family know Latin? Do you know Latin? And those symbols are from occultism." I spoke too soon.

"Charlotte, how do you know this, and why have you been meddling about it?" Ma asked firmly.

"Well, I borrowed some Latin books from the library because I wanted to see what it said. I saw the recipe, eh, spell for eternal life. And I saw that 'as above, so below' is written on the back of Aunty Em's photo. I just wanted to know what it all meant," I said innocently enough. I was half expecting Ma to get angry but wasn't sure where she'd stand on the matter in her good mood.

"Listen, Charlotte. You must not read those scribblings: they **are** from the occult. This family has a rich history. But we are Christians now, and we don't meddle in that nonsense. That's all it is. It's utter nonsense," she reassured me.

"Yes, Ma," I say. I didn't want to push her any further as that's possibly the kindest response I could've gotten from Ma. At least she confirmed that the symbols and writings are Occultism. I just had to find out why they were there.

We happily finished eating breakfast as a family. Then, Ma said the unthinkable. "Let's walk up to the clearing today!"

"But, Ma... I thought it was dangerous. And I saw the grey wolf up there," I told her.

"Don't be silly, Charlotte. It's excellent. There won't be any wildflowers, but who knows what we might find," she said with a huge smile on her face.

We all got our coats and hiking boots on. Ma looked beautiful. She had brushed her hair for the first time in a long time. She was wearing a royal blue sweater and jeans with a deep purple coat. Together, we followed the creek until we made it to the clearing. The cold had ruined the clearing. The grass was dead, and the treeline was bare of leaves. Still, Ma looks very excited to be there. And so do the girls.

"Now, why don't y'all play while I read my book some," she said.

It was a little cloudy out, so it was pretty chilly. I figured that if we played tag that we would warm-up. We were so busy chasing each other and laughing that I hadn't even noticed Ma move from her spot. I looked around until I found her.

She was standing at the edge of the clearing and looking into the forest. Her arms hung lifelessly by her side like heavy weights, and she had her head cocked sharply to the side. It was an eerie sight.

Then I saw it. I saw the grey wolf. It was standing about three feet in front of her. Its eyes still looked cold. It appeared hungry, with saliva dripping from its sharp teeth. And it still looked as though it hadn't eaten anything in a while.

"Ma!" I yelled. I don't think she heard me. I told the girls to stay put, and I ran over to Ma's side. "Ma!" I yelled again. She didn't budge, and her eyes glossed over also. The wolf lowered its head and let out a low growl. I was scared for our lives.

Then Ma's head straightened up quickly with a snapping sound, and the wolf whimpered and ran away.

"What is it, Charlotte?" she asked.

"Ma... the wolf," I said.

"There's no wolf here, " she said, confused.

"Ma, did you not see the wolf that was standing right in front of you?" I cried.

"Charlotte, honey, there was no wolf. See, it's just a stump," she said, pointing to a stump in the forest. I think you must have thought you saw it again. You are probably just worried due to the last time you were here," she said.

"Ma, I want to go home," I said.

"Charlotte, that's nonsense. We just got here," she said.

So, we continued playing in the clearing. The girls seemed to have not even noticed the wolf. This time, Ma joined in by playing tag with us. We also hunted for mushrooms. It seems the winter had claimed those, too, because

69

we came up empty-handed. We also searched for rabbit holes. We found a couple, but there were no signs of rabbits on this cold day. They were probably burrowed beneath the ground.

We were singing "Ring Around the Rosie" with our hands linked together and spinning in a circle when there was a wolf's howl in the distance.

"Ma, I want to go home," I said.

"Well, damn, Charlotte," Ma said. "I guess that wolf is still out here."

So, we made our way home. I laid on my bed, staring at the ceiling. "What is wrong with Ma?" I asked myself. None of this made any sense. And I still had the nagging feeling that something was just not right. Images of Ma banging her head against the wall, sitting erect in her bed, and standing at the edge of the clearing in a lifeless form haunted me. What worried me the most was that Ma wasn't herself today. Sure, it was a nice break from her aloof yet hateful moods. However, Ma wasn't acting like Ma, and that scared me more than anything.

I had no idea what to expect from her anymore, and that was more worrisome than expecting the worst all the time. And how did Ma not see the wolf that was standing right in front of her earlier? Ma was the one who had said that a wolf was a bad omen. Maybe she was right.

Chapter 12

T he following morning, things were back to normal. I took Ma her coffee. She spent the morning lying in bed and watching TV as usual. She primarily watched soap operas. I cleaned the house and took care of the girls. It was as if yesterday had been completely fine, and nothing out of the ordinary had occurred.

I was dusting the living room when I heard a knock on the door. It was Sarah bringing the banana bread that she had promised me.

"Good afternoon, Charlotte," Sarah greeted me.

"Hello, Miss Sarah," I replied.

"How are you and the girls? I have missed seeing you all at church," she inquired.

"We are doing good. We just haven't been because the church bus doesn't run this way in the winter. Even though we haven't had snow, the roads get icy, I guess. And we'd walk into town, but it takes me forever to get the girls ready, so we'd never make it in time," I told her. "By the way, Miss Sarah, I need to talk to you about something."

"Sure, what is it?" she asked.

"Well, I mean, I need to talk to you later at some point. I can't talk here," I said quietly.

"Of course. Come by any time," Sarah said. "Where's your momma? I'd love to see her."

"She is in her room. I'll let her know you are here," I told her.

I went to Ma's room. "Ma, Miss Sarah is here. She brought banana bread," I told her.

Ma gave me a sideways glance, and she said, "That's nice of her. Be sure to tell her thank you."

"I think she was hoping to see you, Ma," I told her. "That's why I came to let you know she is here."

"Dammit, Charlotte. If I wanted to see Sarah, I would give her a visit, or I would have asked her to stop by," she said. "Now, you have put me in an awkward situation. You don't think but for yourself. Tell her I'll be out in a moment."

Great. I managed to make Ma angry first thing this morning. Things were definitely back to normal.

She came out, and I left the room for them to talk, and I put away the banana bread. I heard the door shut after they said their goodbyes, and as soon as it did, Ma appeared in the kitchen with a furious look on her face.

"Charlotte, why have you been telling people of my business?!" she yelled.

"What do you mean, Ma?" I don't even talk to nobody.

"Then why was Sarah concerned about me staying in my room all day?" Ma asked.

"I just told Miss Sarah that I was worried about you!" I said.

It was at that moment that Ma hit me with a closed fist. It was the first time she ever did. I could taste the blood from my lip, and my ears were ringing. I was so shocked that I couldn't even cry. I touched my lip and could feel where Ma had split it. Blood soaked my fingers.

"Loose lips sink ships, Charlotte," Ma said. "I don't want you talking to her anymore."

"But Ma, she is our neighbor and has been your friend for years," I said.

"That's fine and dandy, but since you want to meddle in grown folk business, I think it's best that you not talk to Sarah anymore," she affirmed.

I had no leg to stand on. I was a little angry at Miss Sarah for mentioning it to Ma. But there's no way she would have known that Ma would get so mad about it. I was now second-guessing if I should tell Miss Sarah about yesterday's events and the family Bible like I planned to. But I had to tell somebody. Tuesday was supposed to be a sunny day, so I would make the walk to her house then.

Miss Sarah was very bright. She had been valedictorian of her class. She was also level-headed and logical, so I knew that she'd be able to help me from a nonbias standpoint. I just didn't know what to do anymore with Ma acting bizarre and unpredictable.

I went to my room to examine my lip. It looked like it needed stitches, but there was no way Ma would take me to a doctor for it. I held a paper towel to it to try to stop the bleeding. It was already beginning to bruise as well. It hurt and stung badly.

I scavenged the bathroom medicine cabinet for the liquid bandage. I wasn't sure if you were supposed to use it near your mouth, but my attempts at stopping the bleeding had been futile. I applied it to my lip. It stung, but it stopped the bleeding almost instantly. I then used Neosporin hoping that it would prevent infection or scarring. I didn't need another scar to remember Ma by.

I was sore. My back and legs were still bruised and battered from a couple of days before. My head hurt behind my eyes from lack of solid sleep and stress. And my heart broke most of all. Ma had been getting more and more violent, and there was nothing that I could do to stop it.

Nonetheless, I shook it all off and got ready to homeschool the girls. Today, we were learning about the Presidents. History was my least favorite subject to understand, much less teach. But somebody had to teach the kids.

Here we were, though—all sitting around the kitchen table and getting ready to learn about the nation's Presidents.

"What happened to your lip?" Anna asked.

"Ma *obviously* did it," Sadie responded snarkily.

"Okay, we aren't going to worry about my lip," I said.

"But it looks like it hurts," Anna replied. She had a sad look on her face.

"I think you should put some ice on it," Sadie said.

"Okay, if I put ice on it, can we stop talking about it?" I asked.

"Yes!" Sadie said.

I got up from the table and grabbed a bag of frozen peas from the freezer. Ma came into the kitchen.

"Your lip will be fine," she said stoically. "But I hope you learned your lesson.

You shouldn't be telling anyone my business. If I wanted people to know my business, I would tell them myself."

"Yes, ma'am," I responded.

"After school, I want you to dust the blinds, Charlotte," Ma said. "They're looking awful."

"Yes, ma'am," I replied again.

I didn't want to say or do anything that would piss Ma off again.

She hugged Anna and gave her a high-five for naming the past ten Presidents. Then she left to go back to her room.

I finished up homeschool with the girls, and then I got busy dusting the blinds. I wiped each blind one by one, making sure not to miss a spot. Then I noticed a crow on the mailbox again. This time, it had what looked like a large spider in its beak. While disgusting, I thought that maybe crows were good luck to have around if they eat pesky, creepy spiders. I gave it a wave, and it flew away.

I finished dusting the blinds and sneezed from all the dust. I decided that I would wash the curtains as well, so I put them in the washer. While they soaked, I cleaned the windows. While I was cleaning the last window, Ma came to the living room.

She sang the lyrics to *Cinderelly*.

She always thought it was funny, but I found it to be quite degrading. So, out of instinct, I rolled my eyes. I couldn't help it.

"Don't roll your eyes at me, Charlotte!" she yelled.

She then ran up on me, and I flinched.

"If you think you are grown enough to roll your eyes at me, then be grown enough and do something," she said.

"I didn't mean to roll my eyes, Ma," I said.

"Yeah, right," Ma replied. "So, we don't have control over our facial expressions now?"

I didn't say anything as I didn't want to say the wrong thing.

"Well, when you are done, you can sweep the basement," Ma said.

"Yes, ma'am," I said.

I finished up and then headed down to the basement. When I was sweeping,

I came across an old box labeled "Blackleach Family." Blackleach was Ma's maiden name and her mother's last name. I opened up the box to see what was inside.

Inside, I found an intricate sterling silver jewelry box with a cracked mirror. The only thing inside was a large sapphire amulet on a silver chain. The charm was almost the size of my palm, and it was beautiful. Even though light dimly lit the basement, the amulet still caught what seemed like every light ray, and it sparkled.

I also found an envelope of photos labeled "Blackleach Coven." One photo pictured Grandma and Aunty Em burning bundles of flowers. Another picture was of Grandma and Ma as a child wearing peculiar hats that made them look like witches.

I also found bundles of dried flowers, crystals, and tarot cards in the box. And something that appeared to be the skull of an animal, perhaps a dog. I was in awe of what I found and wanting nothing more than to ask Ma about the box. However, there is no way she would be pleased that I poked around in her things.

I quickly put the contents back in the box and tucked it away where I found it. Then I stumbled upon another box. It was a long, black velvet box. I took the top off and saw the beautiful shimmering royal blue fabric. I pulled it out of the box. It was a hooded cloak. At the shoulders were silver intricately stitched wildflowers.

I put it on and looked in an old wooden mirror that hung on the basement wall. I looked stunning. I twirled around and giggled. But out of fear of being caught by Ma, I put the cloak away and went back to my chores.

I had never stumbled upon the items before because I typically hated the basement and tried to stay out of it. But, now, I wondered what else I would find if I looked around. I finished sweeping the floor and then went back upstairs, where Ma had another small list of chores that needed to be done before dinner. Ma threatened to bust my upper lip if I didn't get it done, so I got straight to work.

Chapter 13

I lied awake that night, contemplating my death.

I couldn't do this anymore. My lip was busted and bruised. I still had bruises on my back from Ma. Every day I was walking on eggshells, and I had no way to defend myself when Ma lashed out at me. I wasn't even sure if she loved me or if I was the bane of her existence.

What kind of child wasn't even loved by their mother? No matter how hard I tried, I couldn't make her happy. Everything I did was essentially for Ma. Still, she was always so furious with me.

It was then that I realized that it wasn't the injuries and bruises that upset me the most. It was the feeling of being unloved and alone. The one person I was supposed to turn to was the same person making me feel so isolated. It was like when Daddy died, I lost my mother, too.

I just wanted to end it all. I wanted peace. I wanted the world to be still. I no longer wanted to be drowning in my own pitiful thoughts. I was ready to be swallowed by the darkness.

Finally, I had the courage. I went to the kitchen, grabbed a knife from the knife block, and went back to my room. I stared at the blade and relished in its glory. It was an old knife Daddy had made. The wooden handle had our family surname, Wardwell, etched into it. I ran my finger along with the etching then along the blade. The sharp edge would help me reach my fate. I imagined the blood slowly draining from me as I drifted off to sleep. At last, I would be at peace. As I pressed the cold, sharp knife against my wrist, I heard Sadie scream.

"Charlotte!! CHARLOTTE!" she screamed.

I quickly hid the knife beneath my pillow and rushed into her room.

"What's wrong?" I asked as I held my arms around her.

She appeared petrified as she slowly pointed to her music box. I hadn't noticed, but the music box was open and playing Symphony No. 5 from Beethoven. The little ballerina twirled around and around in her blush pink tutu. I got up and shut the music box. My family had passed it down for generations. So Ma had given it to Sadie as a gift because she was obsessed with ballet.

"What happened?" I asked.

"The music box started playing by itself," she said.

"Nonsense. It must have been Anna." I said. But as I looked over at Anna, she was sound asleep. "Are you telling a lie, Sadie?"

"Charlotte, I am **not** lying!" she yelled. "Can I sleep with you?"

"Fine. Just give me a second." I told her. I brought her pillows and blanket to my bed. I quickly took the knife back to the kitchen. Then, I went to get Sadie.

"Come on, Sadie," I told her. "Let's get to bed."

"Charlotte, I didn't touch the music box," she whined.

"Okay, kiddo," I replied.

As soon as we crawled into bed, Sadie fell asleep. Whatever had happened, it frightened her greatly. Sadie had been sleeping on her own since she was a baby. And she did not scare easily. So, I was a little shaken myself and couldn't fall asleep. It was an old music box. Perhaps it was broken. But I remembered all the strange things that I had heard and seen. I shuddered.

I laid in bed thinking about what would happen to the girls if I passed away. While I would like to believe that Ma would have to start taking care of them and the house on her own, I thought to myself, "What if Ma forced Sadie to take my role?" Ma may make her be the one to look after Anna and the house. And Sadie may end up being the target of Ma's anger and outbursts. I couldn't let that happen. I had to stay alive for the girls.

Nevermind the trauma of losing a sister to suicide. I am glad Sadie didn't find me in a pool of my blood. Although I felt like an encumbrance to Ma, I knew it was the opposite of the girls. They needed me. And leaving them here would lay a significant burden upon them. I couldn't do that to Anna and Sadie.

I finally drifted off to sleep. I dreamed about the wolf. It was chasing me, and no matter how long I ran, I couldn't make it to the house. My legs felt as heavy as lead, and I was out of breath. I tripped over a tree limb, and the wolf was right on top of me. Saliva was dripping down on my face, and he let out a howl. His jaws opened wide. Then I woke up to a bang.

Something had hit the bedroom window. Then, suddenly, there was another bang. A crow flew right into the window. I grabbed my flashlight and opened up the window to look outside. Lying on the ground were many crows flapping their wings but failing to fly. I didn't know what to do, but Ma would. She was against any creature suffering, well, except her children it seemed. I shone my flashlight in the sky, and a murder of crows was flying in the light.

Bang. BANG.

One by one, crows kept hitting the house. I went to Ma's room, where she was still awake and reading her book.

She looked up at me and asked, "What is all that ruckus?"

"Ma, crows, are flying into the house and hurting themselves," I told her.

"Are you sure, Charlotte?" she asked wearily.

"Yes, Ma. I took a look myself, and they're flapping their wings around on the ground. I don't think they can fly," I said.

Ma walked to my room and looked out the window.

"Yes, they're hurt. And the birds cracked the window," Ma said. "Go get the BB gun, Charlotte. We can't let them suffer."

I grabbed the BB gun, and we headed outside. It was a cold night, but the stars and moon shone brightly, and it was peaceful. The air smelled fresh and of trees. Ma pumped the gun, and then, as I looked away, I heard multiple shots and flinched every time. When I looked back, the crows were no longer moving.

"Charlotte, go get the shovel so we can bury these birds," she said.

"Can't we wait till the morning?" I asked.

"No, it's the right thing to bury them so that scavengers don't get to them," she responded.

I headed to the garden shed to get the shovel. At night, it was a little spooky even for me. Spider webs glistened in the light of my flashlight. The shed smelled of old tools and dirt. I quickly grabbed the shovel so I could get out of there.

Back behind the house, I began digging a shallow grave.

"You know, it's bad luck for crows to fly into your home. Much less, this many crows," Ma said wearily. "Crows are intelligent creatures. They usually bring good luck if you see them. But for them to fly into the house, that's bad. Especially this many. There must be a dozen. That means death is coming."

"Ma, do you believe that?" I asked as I continued to shovel dirt out of the ground.

"I do. It doesn't mean it's coming to our house but to this town," Ma said. "And with this harsh winter, it's no surprise. It's been hard on everybody, I presume."

I was sure Ma was just superstitious again. For a Christian woman, she sure had a lot of superstitions. Undoubtedly, the crows had just gotten lost in the dark or something. But I can't say that it didn't bother me that all of Ma's superstitions lately have been bad ones.

"What was Sadie yelling about earlier?" Ma asked.

"Her music box was playing by itself," I replied, not knowing what else to say.

"That's silly. Sadie must have wound it up," Ma said.

"I don't know, Ma," I said. "She was freaked out. So much that she wanted to sleep in my bed, and Sadie isn't afraid of nothing."

"Maybe it's broken. It is an ancient music box. My great grandmother had it when she was just a little girl," Ma said.

"Maybe so. But Sadie was petrified over the darn thing," I replied. "And so many strange things have been happening."

"Oh, Charlotte, I am sure that it's just coincidence," she said unconvincingly.

Considering Ma was always superstitious, I had a hard time believing that she thought it was all a coincidence or that every single thing had an explanation. So, her affirmation didn't make me feel any better.

I finished digging the hole, and Ma gently placed the crows inside. After I covered them up, she said a short prayer. We stood there for a while, looking at the grave, then headed back into the house.

"Charlotte, I don't want you worrying about those birds," Ma said. "I know how much you love animals. When you found that dead bunny when you were little, you were distraught for days."

"I know, Ma," I said. "But I am not little anymore. I think I can handle it."

"I sometimes forget that you are just about grown now," Ma said with a smile.

I smiled back at her.

"Goodnight, Charlotte," she said.

"Goodnight, Ma," I replied.

I couldn't help but feel a little bad for wanting to kill myself. Of course, Ma was depressed and stressed. All of the bad things would all indeed pass once she got better. She must get better. I also felt like we had bonded a little bit over the burying of birds. Maybe things would get better soon.

Ma hadn't always been as violent and angry as she has been. There was once a time before Daddy died when she was always happy, and you never saw her in a foul mood. But even after Daddy had died, she didn't hit us. That didn't start until recently.

I thought about all of the strange things that had been happening lately. "What if it all wasn't a coincidence?" I asked myself.

Just as strange things had started taking place, Ma had been more aloof, and her temper had gotten worse. What if everything was tied together somehow? The family Bible, Ma, and everything that had happened in the house. I wasn't sure if it was a silly thought or if the birds had shaken me up. I had never seen birds fly into a place like that before. I counted them as Ma had buried them, and there were sixteen. That is a lot of birds.

Tomorrow, I would look at Ma's encyclopedias to see if I could find any relevant information about birds flying into places. Maybe I could head down to the library, too. I pushed the thoughts out of my head and tried hard to get some sleep. Unfortunately, my efforts were futile. It was a very long night of tossing and turning.

Chapter 14

"Ma, I'm going into the forest today. It's nice out," I lied.

"Okay, just be careful," she replied.

Ma was in a good mood and was kinder. I felt terrible lying to her. But I knew that I needed some help with everything that had happened. So, I set off to Miss Sarah's.

Miss Sarah lived about 3 miles up the road, so I rode my bike. It was an old cruiser that Ma had when she was a little girl. In the basket, I had the family Bible and the Latin books. I didn't mind the ride since it was so sunny today.

On the way, I passed the stream. I saw jackrabbits playing in the woods. I heard the sound of birds chirping. It was a gorgeous day outside with the sun shining and the wind still. I would much rather be enjoying it than trying to uncover family secrets.

The ride was silent. Miss Sarah's house was the closest to us, so there was nothing in between. And the road was a dirt road. I was kicking up dust behind me.

I finally made it to Sarah's. Her home was a small cottage with green picket fencing. Her house has ivy growing up the side of it and she has many bushes around her house that just make it look like part of a magical garden. I saw smoke coming from her fireplace.

I knocked on the green arched door and waited for her to answer.

"Hello, Charlotte!" she greeted me. "I am so glad you came by! Come on in!"

I entered her home and was immediately met with the scent of freshly baked bread. Her living room was small but adorable. She had cute wooden furniture with lots of flowers and plants. Throw blankets covered the couch. And her walls were the faintest shade of blush.

We walked down the hall that was covered in pictures of her family. I quickly noticed a beautiful girl with sun-kissed skin and wavy dark brown hair. Miss Sarah caught me admiring the photo, and I blushed.

"That's my niece," She said. "And this is my brother. Oh, look, here is a picture of your mom and me when we were on the high school cheerleading squad. Those were the days."

I giggled. They had giant hair and looked like models from an 80s magazine.

A white Persian cat brushed against my legs.

"Is this Whiskers?!" I exclaimed. Whiskers was a cat that Miss Sarah has had forever.

"Yes, it is! He is still alive. I think cats really do have nine lives," she said.

I bent down to pet Whiskers, but he hissed at me, and the hair on the back of his neck stood up, so I let him be. He used to be so friendly, but maybe he was temperamental in his old age.

She led me to her study. It smelled of oak, leather, and books, much like the library. She had an extensive selection of books. Autobiographies, cookbooks, and non-fiction filled her shelves. I dreamed that one day I would have such a comprehensive collection. Perhaps, in my own bookstore.

"Now, what can I help you with? And what happened to your lip?" she inquired.

I thought about lying to her, but I figured she must know the truth so that she doesn't accidentally let Ma know that I stopped by.

"Well, Ma got angry that I had told you about her staying in her room all the time, and she hit me," I admitted. "She also told me not to talk to you anymore, so she will get furious if she knows I am here."

"Oh my god, Charlotte. I am so sorry. If I had known, I wouldn't have said anything," she apologized. "Does your mother hurt you often?"

"No, she doesn't," I lied. "It was just this time."

"Okay. But you know you can tell me anything," Miss Sarah said.

"I know, Miss Sarah," I said. "But, I really am fine."

"Now, what did you need to talk to me about?" Miss Sarah asked.

"There have been some bizarre things happening, and I need your help," I told her. "Ma has acted strangely. I caught her sleepwalking. I also saw a wolf in the woods. I have heard and seen some people in the house that weren't there. Sadie's music box was playing by itself."

I was talking faster than I could even think.

"Slow down, Charlotte," Miss Sarah said. "There has to be an explanation for everything."

"Will you just take a look at the family Bible for me?" I asked.

She flipped through it and confirmed that it was the writings of the occult.

"Oh, I studied symbols like these in college when I studied Occultism," she said excitedly.

She pulled some books from her shelf. One heavy book had "Demonology" written across the front.

We spent about ten minutes in silence as she flipped through books and referred back to the family Bible. She looked intrigued and like she was having a fabulous time trying to decipher the words and symbols in the Bible.

Finally, she said, "It appears that your family was involved in the Occult for some time. There is a spell of Eternal Life. After completing the spell, you must submit yourself to Astorath."

"Who is Astorath?" I asked.

"It seems that Astorath is a fallen angel or a demon," she said. "He is part of the evil trinity right up there with Lucifer. If the person does not submit to him by their 30th birthday, then he will come for their soul, and they will suffer eternal damnation."

I looked at her wide-eyed and must have alarmed her.

"Charlotte, you know this stuff is fake and born from long-lived myths, right?' Sarah said.

"But it makes sense with everything that has happened. Ma just had her 30th birthday, and I think Ma is in trouble," I replied.

"No, I think you are just under a lot of stress, and you are looking for reasons why Ma hasn't been well aside from just normal grieving," she said.

"Great," I thought to myself. "Sarah doesn't believe me."

"What else is in the Bible?" I asked.

"There are recipes for various spells and oils and concoctions, mostly derived from wildflowers," Sarah explained. "It seems this Bible has been in your family since the 18th century."

"Why would anyone involved with the Occult have a Bible?" I asked.

"Well, with the persecution of witches, many that practiced the occult pretended to be Christians," she replied. "Over time, some people practiced both. They became Christian witches of a sort."

"So is my family a bunch of witches?" I asked.

"I wouldn't go that far," she replied. "Even if they were witches at one point, your momma is a good Christian woman."

"What if my house is haunted?" I asked.

"Charlotte, honey, your house isn't haunted," she said. "Not that I believe in those sorts of things but, if anyone thought it was haunted, I would have known. I have lived here my whole life, just like your family, and this town talks."

"Well, Miss Sarah, I have to get back before Ma gets worried. I told her that I was heading into the forest today," I said.

I gathered my belongings and headed to the door.

"Charlotte, if you need **anything** at all, please don't hesitate to come by," she said.

"I won't," I responded.

"Okay then. Take care. I'll see you later," Miss Sarah said.

"Bye, Miss Sarah," I responded.

On the way home, I rode much slower. Why didn't anyone believe me? I know that I had not imagined the man at Sadie's bedside. Something was wrong, and if Ma somehow wrapped herself up in the occult, that would explain everything. However, there was nothing more that I could do.

When I got home, Ma was making dinner. She was making her infamous shrimp salad. It was a salad full of shrimp, spinach leaves, and bacon. She was humming her favorite song, November Rain. She seemed to be in a very cheerful mood.

I slumped down in a chair at the kitchen table. I was dog-tired physically and mentally.

"What's wrong?" Ma asked.

"I didn't sleep well last night," I half-fibbed.

"Oh, darling. Why don't I make you some tea," she offered.

"Sure," I said.

Ma got the copper-colored teapot out of the cabinet and put the water on. She had her herbal tea mixtures, so I requested the winter solstice tea. It tasted like peppermint candy and was so comforting. Even the smell of it brewing relaxed me.

"Ma, can I ask you about the family Bible?" I asked cautiously.

"No, Charlotte, you may not," she replied.

I impatiently said, "But Ma, I want to know more about the drawings and the other things that are in there."

"Charlotte, that's enough," she said. "Maybe one day, I will tell you about it when you are older, but I don't want you prying around it now. And you said you would stop looking into it."

"Yes, ma'am," I said.

"How was your trip to the woods?" she asked.

"My trips to the woods?" I asked, confused.

"Yes, silly," she responded. "The trip to the woods you just took. You really must be exhausted."

"Oh! It was good. Nothing strange happened, but the cold has ruined the woods," I responded. "Everything is dead and gone."

"Here's your tea," she said, sitting the warm cup down at the table.

"After we eat dinner, why don't you take a warm bath to help you sleep," she said.

"That's a great idea," she said.

After dinner, I ran my bathwater. I always took showers, so the thought of soaking in the bath was lovely. I slid into the tub and laid back. I focused on the soothing sound of the dripping faucet. The warm water wrapped around me like a blanket. I submerged under the water to get my hair wet. For a second, I wondered what would happen if I didn't come back up for air. When I came back up, I saw a shadowy figure on the other side of the shower curtain.

"Chaaarlotte."

I heard the same venomous voice that I had heard in Sadie's room.

I sat straight up in the bath and yanked the shower curtain back. I looked around, but I didn't see anyone there. I suddenly felt freezing, and I no longer wanted to be alone. I made my way out of the tub and quickly got dressed. I was too afraid to sleep in my room, so I climbed into bed with Anna. She did not mind the company. After telling her the story of *Hansel and Gretel* for the 100th time, she finally fell asleep.

I felt long fingers wrap around my throat, and then I saw him. The tall, shadowy man was on top of me, and I couldn't breathe.

"You are worthless, you little brat!" he said. "Do you hear me? You are worthless!"

I struggled to break free, but the more I fought, the tighter his grasp became.

"Charlotte, your life means nothing," he hissed. "Your mother hates you and wants you to diiie!"

I felt my circulation being cut off from my head and thought I was going to pass out.

"Charlotte!" Anna cried. "Charlotte!"

Suddenly, the man was gone, and I saw Anna's terrified face.

"Charlotte, you were having a nightmare," Anna said, worried.

"Oh, praise the Lord, it was just a nightmare," I said breathlessly.

"Are you okay?" Anna asked.

"Yes, I am fine," I said. "Thank you for waking me up."

Anna rolled back over to go back to sleep. I stared at the ceiling for the rest of the night. The nightmare had felt so real. I thought I was going to die.

Chapter 15

The next morning, I woke with sore ribs. I pulled up my shirt, and there was a large purple bruise on my side. I checked it out in the girls' mirror.

I went to take Ma her coffee, and I showed her my bruise.

"Ma, I woke up with this giant bruise on my side," I said.

"Oh my god, Charlotte," Ma said. "Are you okay?"

"Yes, I am okay, but isn't that a bit weird to you?" I asked, puzzled as to why Ma wasn't as alarmed as I was.

"Not really," Ma said. "You slept with Anna on a twin size bed. She probably just whacked you in her sleep or something."

"If you say so," I told Ma. "What are you up to today?"

"I am thinking we girls can all have a spa day!" Ma said excitedly. "I'll get all of my makeup out, and we can do our makeup and paint our nails."

"Oh, that sounds like so much fun!" I exclaimed.

It had been a while since Ma had worn makeup. And it had been even longer since we had a spa day. I left to go to the kitchen to make the girls breakfast when I heard a knock on the door.

I peered out the peephole and saw a plump little woman in a pantsuit and some kind of a badge. She had short red hair and a round little face. I opened the door.

"Yes, can I help you?" I asked.

"Oh, hello. You must be Charlotte. I am looking to speak with your mother, Luna Blackleach," she said half out of breath. "I am from Child Protection Services."

"Just a moment, and I will go get her," I said.

"Ma, there is a woman from Child Protection Services here, and she wants to speak to you," I told Ma. She looked at me, worried.

Ma went into the living room and asked me to leave them to talk. I left them in the living room to talk. Then after a while, the CPS lady asked to speak to me.

"I am Dottie McIntosh, and I am from Child Protection Services," she said.

"Yes, I saw that," I said flatly.

"I am here today because I got a report of child abuse," she said. "What happened to your lip, Charlotte?"

"I was mopping, and I slipped on the kitchen floor," I lied.

"Charlotte, you know you can trust me," she said calmly. "Has your mother ever hit you?"

"No, she has not," I lied again.

I repeatedly lied as she asked me questions about my relationship with Ma and told me of any allegations. The only person who had seen us lately was Miss Sarah, so I knew she had to be the one that called. I was worried how Ma, who had been in an excellent mood for three straight days, would react.

"What about homeschool?" she asked.

"What about it?" I replied angrily.

"Who teaches Anna and Sadie?" she asked.

"Well, I usually go over their school work with them," I admitted. "We do our school work together."

"I see," she said, scribbling in her notebook. "And who teaches you, Charlotte?"

"I teach myself," I said.

"You teach yourself?" she peered up at me from her notebook.

"Yes. I teach myself," I insisted. "I am competent. I have taught myself Spanish, and I am almost fluent."

"Okay, that's all I have for you," Dottie said.

"Yes, ma'am. I'll see you out." I told her.

I walked her to the door, where she gave me a card and told me to call her if I needed anything at all. I was both angry and scared.

"Ma, what was that all about? Are you in trouble?" I asked wearily.

"No, I am not in trouble. I don't want you to worry, but Dottie will be conducting monthly visits. We have to keep the house as clean as possible, and we can't have any more issues," she said.

"Okay. What do I need to do?" I asked.

"Just help me keep the house clean and be on your best behavior," she said. "Oh, and I think it was Sarah that called. That's why I am glad you aren't speaking to her anymore."

I felt my cheeks flush. It was my fault that Child Protection Services had gotten called. I should have never told Miss Sarah what had happened. If Ma loses her temper anymore, there is no telling what trouble she'd get into and what would occur to us girls. I was also slightly flustered that Ma seemed to think that I wasn't always on my best behavior. But that was the least of my concerns for now.

"This is just the stress I didn't need," Ma said to herself. "Right when things are going good."

"I'm sorry, Ma," I said.

"Well, Charlotte, there is nothing to be sorry about," Ma said.

I felt even worse. Ma had no idea that it was indeed my fault, and I had everything to be sorry about.

I cleaned the house from top to bottom, mostly out of guilt. I did loads of laundry. I dusted baseboards and window sills. I even cleaned the musty old basement. It was creepy down there, and I hated cleaning the cobwebs. But I knew that the house had to be in tip-top shape, so I did what I had to do.

I know that Ma had messed up lately, but I didn't want my family torn apart. We had already been through enough together with the death of Daddy. And I needed to be there for my sisters.

While in the basement, I stumbled across more boxes labeled *Blackleach*. I didn't meddle in them as I didn't want to cause any more trouble. I couldn't let my curiosity get the best of me.

After I cleaned the house, I headed to the library. Luckily, it was open, but the librarian was still out. I made my way to the section with books on crows.

Finally, I found a large book with tons of information.

After reading through the book, I stumbled upon a page dedicated to explaining omens and odd occurrences with crows. Again, it was confirmed that people believed that crows flying into your house were signs of death. Apparently, crows were considered messengers. The crows themselves weren't evil but could be messengers for maleficent entities.

I shuddered and closed the book, putting it back on the shelf. I rode home on my bike. It was a grey day with dark, ominous clouds in the sky. I wasn't sure if they looked extra spooky or if my nerves were just worked up. I pedaled home as fast as I could.

When I got home, I decided to cheer up Ma by getting ready for our spa day. I got large Tupperware containers for us to soak our feet in. I got Ma's face mask from the bathroom, as well as her fingernail polishes, and I made a pitcher of lemonade. Then, I went to get her.

"Ma, are you ready for our spa day?" I asked.

"Oh, I don't know if I feel like it, Charlotte," she said.

"I think it would make you feel better," I said in a sing-song voice.

"Oh, alright," she said with a grin. "Get the girls, and I will grab my makeup."

We put on *The Black Cauldron,* and we continued with a spa day. We all did a face mask and braided each other's hair. Ma painted our nails and toenail, and she gave everyone a makeover with her makeup.

"Charlotte, all you will need when you get older is a little bit of eye makeup," Ma said. "Your complexion is just great, and you don't need much else."

It was the first compliment I had received from Ma in a long time. I looked in the mirror and was shocked at how grown I looked. Ma had put bronze eyeshadow on me to make my grey eyes pop. She put just a little bit of liner and mascara and a nude lipstick that, somehow, made my thin top lip slightly a little plumper. I felt beautiful.

Speaking of which, she looked absolutely stunning. She wore an emerald green shirt with scarlet red lipstick. And she gave herself a golden smokey eye, which made her hazel eyes pop. And her dark auburn hair was braided down her back like a queen.

After we finished, Ma asked me to help her make chicken and dumplings.

She hadn't taught me how yet, so I was excited.

"First, we must boil the chicken and make some broth," she said. "While I do that, you make the biscuit dough."

I sifted the flour and combined all the ingredients just how Ma had taught me. When I finished making Ma's homemade biscuits, she showed me how to pinch off just enough for the dumplings. Then I dropped them into the creamy broth one by one. I was excited to be learning a new recipe from Ma like the good ole days.

We all had dinner together. Then Ma finally gave in when the girls begged Ma that we all had a sleepover in the living room. We pulled the mattresses off the girls' beds and dragged them into the living room. We made blanket forts for each bed. We brought in fairie lights from the basement and strung them up in the forts. The forts looked magical. Ma was going to sleep with Anna, and I was going to sleep with Sadie.

Before bed, Ma sang us songs from her childhood, such as "How Much Is That Puppy In The Window." We joined in and giggled together. It was such a sweet moment. She also told us the story of *Little Red Riding Hood*, except in Ma's version, the wolf didn't eat grandma, and he was simply misunderstood. The wolf was more like a playful, big dog in Ma's story.

After Ma sang songs and told us the story, we said our goodnights.

"Goodnight, girls," Ma said.

"Goodnight, Ma," we all said in unison.

It was about 1 am when Sadie and I heard a rustling and saw a shadow outside our fort.

"Ma!" we cried. "Ma! There's something outside of the fort!"

Ma didn't respond.

"Sadie, sit right here," I told her.

I pulled back the blanket to the entry of the fort and was immediately startled. Ma was standing lifelessly in the dark, without clothes. I immediately shielded my eyes.

"Ma!" I cried.

But she still didn't respond.

I looked back at her, and her eyes were glazed over, and her head was cocked to the side. I noticed days-old cut marks on her breasts. There was crimson blood dripping from between her legs, making a puddle on the floor.

I quickly grabbed a blanket and threw it over Ma to cover her. I shook her shoulder gently.

"Ma," I said. "I think you are sleepwalking."

She didn't budge.

"Ma, you have to wake up!" I shook her harder.

"Yes, Charlotte?" she asked.

"Ma, you are sleepwalking," I said.

"Oh my god," she said. "I am so embarrassed!"

Ma ran out of the room to get dressed and clean herself up. I grabbed bleach water and a rag from the kitchen to clean up the blood. I was wiping the floor the best that I could, and then Ma came back into the living room.

"Charlotte, I've got this," she said.

"Ma, it's okay," I replied.

"I've got it!" she snapped. "Go back to bed."

So I went back to the blanket fort with Sadie.

"What was wrong with Ma?" Sadie asked.

"She was just sleepwalking," I said. "Now, let's just go back to sleep."

I held Sadie for the rest of the night.

Chapter 16

The next morning, we woke up, and Ma was gone. She left a note by the coffee pot that read:

Dear Charlotte,

I have some things that I needed to sort out, so I had to leave. I am not sure when I will be back, so be sure to take care of the girls. There is money for groceries in my dresser. I have called your Aunt Cindy to come stay with you.

Love, Mom

I was in shock. Where would Ma possibly have gone? How long was she going to be gone? So many questions swirled in my head. And now Ma left me to take care of the girls without knowing when she would be back.

I made myself some coffee. I hadn't been sleeping well, and I needed it if I was going to seize the day. Sadie came into the kitchen.

"Where's Ma," she asked.

"Well, I'm not sure, but she had some things to take care of, and she will be gone for a little bit," I replied.

"Okay. Can I have some Fruity Pebbles?" she asked.

"Of course," I replied.

I got the big white bowls out of the cabinet and poured three bowls of Fruity Pebbles for the girls and me. We ate breakfast together, and then we planned out our day. We would start by playing with some Play-Doh. Anna made a pink and purple flower, Sadie made a green and yellow snake, and I made a white bunny. I loved bunnies and missed the one I had, Marshmallow, as a small child. Ma had said that they brought good luck.

After that, we went outside and played. We played cops and robbers. We jumped rope. We played on the playset, and the girls took turns letting me push them on the swing. We laughed when Anne slid down the slide on her belly and landed face first in the grass.

After lunch, I rode into town to get milk and eggs. It started snowing out, so I had to hurry before the weather got too bad. While at the corner store, I ran into Miss Sarah.

"Hi, Charlotte. How are you and the girls?" she asked.

"We are fine, Miss Sarah. But I know that you called CPS," I confronted her.

"Honey, I had to do what I had to do. You have a busted and bruised lip, and you are so stressed out," she countered.

"Well, that's just one more thing Ma has to worry about, and she has been doing good," I said.

"Forgive me, Charlotte," she said. "One day, you will understand. Speaking of your momma, where is she? She usually comes into town for the groceries."

I lied, "She is at home feeling a little under the weather. So I came into town for her. I think she might have the flu."

"Oh, okay," Sarah said. "Just don't be too long. It's supposed to get real nasty this afternoon."

"I won't," I said. "I am just grabbing milk and eggs. But I better get going."

"Okay, I will see you around, Charlotte," Miss Sarah said. "And if you or your mom need anything, please don't hesitate to ask."

"See ya," I replied.

I felt a little bad for being short with Miss Sarah, but I was still mad at her. She had no place to get involved with my family's matters the way she did. She should have, at least, tried to talk to Ma first.

I grabbed my milk and eggs and checked out. Then I headed home. About halfway home, the snow began to pick up, so I pedaled faster. I could hardly see, and I almost hit a deer that was standing in the middle of the road. I wrecked my bike, and the groceries went flying. My heart was beating out of my chest. A couple of eggs broke, but, thankfully, most had stayed intact.

By the time I made it home, it had already snowed an inch. It was unbelievable. I put away the milk and eggs and began to make dinner for the girls. Tonight, we were just having a Digiorno pizza. Just as we sat down to eat, I heard a knock at the door,

"Hello, Charlotte!" Bobby said.

"Hey, Bobby," I replied. "Ma's not home."

"Well, I brought a new dryer belt for her," he said. "Why don't ya let me in to replace it."

"Okay," I said reluctantly.

"When's your momma gonna be back?" Bobby asked.

"I'm not really sure," I replied. I grabbed the note from the kitchen and showed Bobby. It wasn't like he'd tell anybody.

"Well, that sure is odd," Bobby said. "But you know her hands are full with you girls. Your momma is a good woman, Charlotte. She tries really hard to take care of ya'll."

"I know, Bobby," I said. "I try to help her the best I can."

"I know you do," he replied. "You're a damn good kid. You got a solid head on your shoulders."

"Thanks, Mister Bobby," I said.

"Oh, Charlotte," Bobby said with a grin. "You've got great manners, young lady, but there ain't no reason to call me Mister Bobby. I'm just Bobby or Bob to you, ya hear?"

"Gotcha," I said, forcing a smile.

Maybe Bobby wasn't so bad. And it felt great to tell *somebody* that Ma was gone. Bobby fixed the dyer right up and then left after giving the girls a high-five or two. He even offered to come by and check on us, but I politely declined.

I tried to call Aunt Cindy but the phone line was down. No doubt it was due to the storm that rolled in. I sent the girls to bed after their nightly bath, and I settled in on the couch to watch *The Shining*.

Just as the movie was getting good, the power went out. The winter storm was undoubtedly the cause. The wind was howling outside, and it was even lightning. I lit some candles and took the girls extra blankets to keep warm.

I was reading in the candlelight when I began to hear the girls laughing. I went to their room with a candle, but they were in bed fast asleep. I heard laughter again, this time coming from the hall. As I headed to the entrance, I heard tiny footsteps running on the wooden floors toward Ma's room.

I held on to my candle and entered Ma's room, but there was nobody there. Just as I turned around to leave, I heard it.

"GET OUT!" a woman's voice said.

The flame of my candle suddenly extinguished. I spun around, my heart racing, but nothing met me. Then Ma's vanity chair flung across the room. It hit the wall and broke into pieces.

"Get out!!" the voice said again.

I still didn't see anyone. Then, a strong breeze blew through the room. With the corner of my eye, I saw it. The wind had blown Ma's curtain, and it caught on what looked like a person standing in the corner of her room. I screamed.

Sadie came rushing into the room, and then the door slammed behind her. Sadie jumped. We tried opening the door, but it was jammed. We couldn't get out of the room. So, we opened Ma's window and jumped down on the ground.

It was freezing outside, and snow was swirling around us as it fell heavily from the sky. We ran to my bedroom window since the front door was locked. Luckily, my window wasn't locked, and we were able to climb back through.

"What was that?" Sadie said, out of breath.

"I- I don't know," I stuttered.

"Something is in Ma's room," Sadie said. "What is it?"

"I don't know, Sadie," I said. "Let's just go back to bed, okay? And try not to wake your sister."

"Okay, Charlotte," Sadie said wearily. "But can you sleep in our room?"

"Of course," I said.

So, I carefully climbed in bed with Anna. For the rest of the night, I could hear the pitter-patter of tiny feet running through the house. This time, however, I stayed in bed.

Chapter 17

The next day, I was exhausted. There wasn't enough coffee to help me. I had slept like shit. I had bags under my eyes, and I looked about five years older than I was. My hair was a mess, and I hadn't changed clothes in two days.

According to Anna, the girls were *starving*, so they wanted more than just cereal, which was unfortunate for me. I tiredly made them eggs and toast. I was half-asleep, standing at the counter, when the pop of the toaster nearly scared me half to death. I was not only sleepy, but I was also extra jumpy this morning.

I gave the kids their breakfast, and I sat at the table drinking my black coffee. I was contemplating what we should do for the day. I didn't have the energy to do much. So, I figured I would let the girls draw for a bit before starting on schoolwork.

The power was back on and the phone line was working again so I called Aunt Cindy. We talked briefly as she was busy. She said that she would come as soon as possible but she was having a hard time finding a flight in with the winter storms that were forecasted to hit our area. Just as I was hanging up, I heard Sadie yell.

"Charlotte! Anna is choking!" Sadie yelled in a panic.

Anna was blue in the face and gasping for air. I quickly did the Heimlich maneuver on her and out popped a black crystal. She was crying.

"Anna! Where did you get this?" I asked.

"I don't know! I didn't have it!" she cried.

"What do you mean you didn't have it?" I asked.

"I was just sitting here, and I started choking!" she exclaimed.

"Did you get it from Ma's room?" I demanded.

"No, Charlotte! I have never seen this crystal, and I don't go into Ma's room!" she said.

I quickly took the crystal to Ma's room and put it on the shelf with her others. It was an obsidian crystal that Ma said was for protection. Then I noticed Ma's diary sitting on her shelf. I knew it was an invasion of privacy, but I wanted to see what she had been writing.

I opened her journal and was immediately horrified. There was an ink drawing of the man I saw standing over Sadie's bed. There were also other drawings of scary creatures to include what looked like something demonic. On one page, "knock, knock" was written over and over about a hundred times in red ink.

I quickly shut the diary and placed it back on the shelf. As I backed away from the shelf, it flew across the room, barely missing me. I ran out of the room as fast as I could and shut the door. But I heard a "knock, knock, knock" coming from the other side.

I slowly opened the door, but nobody was there. Lying at the foot of the doorway was Ma's journal. It was opened to a page with Ma's writing. It read:

I beat Charlotte today. I have told her not to backtalk me so many times. I didn't mean to lose control, but I am not sure what came over me. It was like a blackout. I am pretty sure Charlotte hates me now if she didn't already. She should have just kept her mouth shut! She has no idea how hard it is to lose the love of your life and to be left taking care of ungrateful children. Maybe she deserved to be beat. I bet she won't backtalk me again. She doesn't understand how much she irks me. She just never shuts up!

Tears filled my eyes. It hurt me that Ma thought I hated her, but it hurt me even more that she didn't seem sorry for the day she had left me black and blue. Nonetheless, the girls needed not to see Ma's diary. It would scare them, at least, and probably hurt them as much as it hurt me. I didn't want to read anymore, so I tossed the diary on the bed. I swiftly went to the living room and gathered the girls.

"Listen, you cannot go into Ma's room while she is away," I warned.

"But I didn't go in there," Anna said.

"Listen, Anna. I believe you. I am not saying that you did," I reassured her. "I am just saying to keep Ma's door shut."

"When will Ma be back?" Anna asked.

"Sweetie, I don't know," I said. "She just has some things to take care of. Hopefully, she will be back soon."

"But I miss her," Anna said.

"I know you do," I told her. "How about we make some chocolate chip pancakes for brunch?"

That cheered Anna right up. As the scent of warm chocolate and pancake batter filled the house, I finally felt some sense of peace. Cooking was possibly one of my favorite ways to escape. And I loved when cooking made the house smell so cozy.

I was placing the girls' plates on the table when Sadie came to me.

"Charlotte, that black stone is back on the coffee table," she said.

"What do you mean?" I asked. "Did Anna go get it?"

"No, we didn't go in Ma's room," she said. "We were just playing, and I saw it."

I went to the living room and grabbed the black crystal. I marched right back to Ma's room to return it to her other crystals. When I opened the door, I stood there shocked. Ma's crystals were all a few feet in the air. Suddenly, they dropped.

I screamed.

The girls came running in to ask what had happened. I quickly tried to compose myself.

"It was n-nothing," I stuttered.

"It doesn't seem like nothing," Sadie said.

"Girls, just get out and don't come back in here," I said.

They left, and I reached for Ma's bedroom key above the door frame. I locked the door and put the key in my pocket. Whatever was going on needed to stop. I was exhausted and had no idea what to do. I couldn't ask for Sarah's help, but even if I could, she wouldn't believe me anyway.

For the rest of the day, I was on edge. Thankfully, nothing else strange happened, though. I laid on the couch for most of the day while the girls played. Eventually, there was a knock on the door. It was Miss Sarah.

"Hi, Charlotte!" Miss Sarah said. "Can I come in?"

"Sure," I said. "What do you want?"

"Okay, I see you're still mad at me," she said. "Is your mom around?"

"No, she had to go into town," I lied.

Then I heard Ma's bedroom door slam open. I went to inspect. I wasn't sure how it came unlocked, but the key was in the middle of the hallway. I quickly shut the door and relocked it.

"What was that?" Miss Sarah inquired.

"It was just the wind blowing the door open," I fibbed.

"Oh, okay," Miss Sarah said. "I was just bringing over some freshly baked bread. I made too much and thought I would share."

"Is that all?" I asked with a yawn.

"No," Miss Sarah confessed. "I also wanted to apologize. I realize that maybe I should have talked to your mother before going to social services. I know she's been grieving, and we all deal with grief differently. I was just worried about you, Charlotte. You seem so stressed lately."

"Well, I am fine," I lied again. "Ma has been doing a lot better. Things have seemed to get back to normal a bit. She has been pretty happy, and I can take care of myself."

"Charlotte, I know you can take care of yourself," Miss Sarah said. "But I don't think you should have to. I just want you to know that you can trust me, and you can come to me any time that you ever need something."

"Okay," I replied. "Thank you, Miss Sarah." I didn't quite believe her. Was she genuinely apologetic? Sure. Could I absolutely trust her? I didn't think so, and I couldn't risk her running off to Dottie.

"You are welcome, Charlotte," she said. "I am going to head home now, but if you need me, I am just a phone call away."

"Okay, I will see you later, then," I said as I walked her to the door.

"Bye, Charlotte," she said.

For the rest of the day, I was exhausted and weary. We occasionally heard noises coming from Ma's room. But I was too tired to deal with it, so I tried my best to ignore it. When it came to bedtime, I made a pallet on the living room floor with the girls because I was too afraid to sleep alone.

Chapter 18

Thankfully, the night had been rather quiet except for the sound of footsteps. I had been able to get a little more sleep, though I was still exhausted. My back ached from sleeping on the living room floor. I had an idea. I headed to the basement door and made my way down the old wooden steps. They creaked beneath my feet as I walked down. The basement was dimly lit by the morning sun. I pulled the light switch and turned on the basement light so that I could see better.

I went to the boxes that I stumbled across a couple days ago. I began opening them one by one and couldn't believe my eyes. It seemed that my family had indeed been witches at some point.

I found one box of what appeared to be witch's hats. I tried one on and looked in the mirror. I was amazed and felt at home. Why had Ma kept this away from me?

I found dolls made of straw and dressed in rags. They each had names on them. Some were bound in small chains. Others were pierced by pins. They looked peculiar and gave me the shivers.

Another box contained a small cauldron the size of a mortar. I pulled out books of handwritten spells. I flipped through one of the books. There was a love spell calling for red candles, rose petals, and other supplies. My eyes lit up.

Then, I stumbled across an old photo album. Ma was a small child twirling in the forest clearing. Wildflowers filled the clearing. In another photo, Grandma was burning a bundle of wildflowers with a smile on her face.

Then I came across a book titled, "Book of Dark Arts". Inside were spells for revenge, curses for causing pain, and other seemingly evil spells. I was in awe but cautious. Had my family used these?

I also stumbled across ledgers and other records. One page listed about thirty different women. Ma, Grandma, and Aunty Em were among the list of names. At the bottom of the list I found my own name. I traced my fingers along the letters and could feel my body getting warm. Was I once a witch? Was this my destiny?

"Charlotte?" Sadie called my name, making me jump. I hadn't heard her come into the basement. "What is all this?"

"Oh, it's nothing," I lied.

"It doesn't look like nothing," Sadie insisted. "Ma would kill you if she knew you were going through her things."

"Well, I guess its a good thing Ma isn't here then," I snapped.

Sadie rolled her eyes and asked, "Are those witch hats?"

"I am not sure," I admitted. "It does look like it."

"Why would Ma have witch hats?" she inquired.

"I honestly have no idea," I lied again. Sadie didn't need to know everything that I had found out- not yet, anyway. She was too young to understand. I didn't even understand any of it myself.

I heard the phone ring upstairs.

"Sadie, can you go answer the phone?" I asked. "I will be up in just a minute."

I carefully put everything back in their boxes and put the boxes back in place. You could tell I had disturbed them from the dust but hopefully Ma wouldn't notice when she got back. I turned around to head back upstairs and that is when I saw her.

A shadowy woman dressed in black stood by the stairs with her eyes locked onto mine. She was crying tears of black substance. Her skin was pale white and her long black raven hair flowed down to her waist. I wanted to scream or to run but I stood frozen in fear.

"You're in danger," she cried. And she disappeared into a cloud of fog as quickly as she had appeared. Chills ran down my spine and I shivered. I quickly ran up the tairs and shut the basement door behind me.

I met with Sadie in the kitchen, who was laughing and giggling on the phone. I knew immediately that it had to be Aunt Cindy. Sadie gave me the phone.

"Hello?" I answered.

"Charlotte!" Aunt Cindy exclaimed. "I've got great news! I will be there tomorrow!"

"That's great!" I told Aunt Cindy. "Peculiar and scary things have been happening."

"Well, just hang in there, kiddo," she said. "I'll see you tomorrow. Now I need to get off here to pack."

"Okay," I replied. "We will see you when you get here!"

I hung up the phone and felt relieved. Aunt Cindy would be able to keep us safe.

Chapter 19

For two weeks, I fed the girls. I played with them. I bathed them. I cleaned the house. I took care of everything myself. We dealt with bumps in the night, and the day, coming from Ma's room. However, I forbid the girls, and myself, from checking it out. I barely slept each night and was exhausted. I had wanted to give up. I wanted to ride over to Miss Sarah's house and tell her everything. Luckily, right as I was ready to give in, I heard a knock on the door. Thankfully, it was Aunt Cindy.

Aunt Cindy had olive, tan skin like Ma. But she had bleach blonde hair and dark brown eyes. She had a womanly shape, much unlike Ma's petite figure. Ma had said Aunt Cindy had plastic surgery to be more marketable.

"Aunt Cindy! You are finally here!" I cried. It had been a couple of years since we had seen her.

"Well, I got a call from your mom, and she needed my help," she said. "I'm here to help you take care of the kiddos for a bit."

"Did you fly in?" I asked.

"I sure did. Driving from California to Tennessee is just too much for me!" she laughed. "I grabbed a rental car at the airport."

"How long will you be here?" I inquired.

"Well, I will be here at least a week. Your mom is coming back tomorrow evening," she said. "I'll stay as long as she needs me to."

"What about work?" I asked. Aunt Cindy was a B-list actress that spent all her time in Los Angeles trying to make it big.

"Oh, that can wait! I'd give up the moon to be here with you, girls!" she exclaimed. She tickled me. Aunt Cindy always treated me like one of the kids.

While I was used to being treated more like an adult with Ma, it was a warm welcome.

I laughed and asked, "So what have you been working on?"

"Oh, just some small budget horror movie. We got it wrapped up last week. It comes out next Spring. I am hoping it will lead me to my big break, but we will see!" she said.

"I can't believe my Aunt is a movie star," I said gleefully.

"Now, what do you need help with?" she asked. "The house looks great. You've kept good care of it."

"The biggest thing I need help with is groceries. Ma left us enough money. However, I can only fit a few items in my bike basket, so I have had to go into town nearly every day for something," I replied.

"Easy peasy, lemon squeezy!" she said. "Make me a list, and I'll head into town tonight to the Piggly Wiggly."

"Awesome!" I said. "Let me go get the girls, so they'll know you're here."

I went and told the girls that Aunt Cindy was here to stay with us for a week. They were as excited as I was. They ran into the living room to give her huge hugs and lots of kisses.

"Oh my goodness! You two have gotten so big!" she said to them.

They giggled, and everyone was so happy. Having Aunt Cindy around, even if I was managing without her, would be a huge breath of relief. She always made things more fun. And the fact that Ma was coming home tomorrow was excellent. She and Aunt Cindy always had a great time together. Maybe all the weird things happening would settle down, too.

"Girls, why don't you let me talk to Charlotte for a bit," she said.

The girls ran back to their room to play.

"Charlotte, your mom told me things have been rough around here," she said in a sobering tone. "She told me about your lip. And about Child Protection Services."

"Yes, well, Ma has been very depressed since Daddy died," I said. "She was doing very well for a few days until CPS came by. Then the next morning, she was just gone."

"Yeah, CPS coming by was the last thing your mom needed," she said. "After that, I think she felt like she failed you girls and just needed some time to sort out your thoughts. She also told me that strange things have been happening. I wasn't sure what to make of it."

"Really? Because I am pretty sure Ma didn't believe me one bit when I saw a figure in the girls' room," I said. "So many weird things have been happening, and I have been trying to figure it all out. I haven't slept well in weeks. I also did some research on the family Bible and…"

"About that," Aunt Cindy cut me off. "Your mom and I have discussed the family Bible and all of that. We think it's time you know the deep history of our family and what we think is happening."

"Well, what *is* happening?" I asked.

"I don't want to discuss it until your mom comes home tomorrow. There is just so much to discuss, and I think it's important that your mom be here for it. Then, we will sit down together to talk about it," she assured me.

"Okay, then," I said. I was honestly excited to finally get some answers, even if that meant having to wait one more night. "I am going to make some fried bologna sandwiches for lunch. Do you want one?"

"Of course I want one!" she laughed. "We don't get southern cooking in Los Angeles. And I will be happy to assist."

We headed to the kitchen where Aunt Cindy put mayo on bread and cut the tomatoes. I fried the bologna. I couldn't believe some people found bologna atrocious. I thought it was delicious, and the smell of it frying in the pan brought back great memories of watching both my Grandma and Ma frying bologna. We mostly had fried bologna sandwiches on warm summer days, but I was over the cold and needed something to remind me of hotter weather.

We all merrily ate at the kitchen table. When I finished, I made a lengthy grocery list for Aunt Cindy. I was happy that we would have some variety back in the kitchen instead of the milk, eggs, and sandwiches we had been living off while Ma was gone.

While Aunt Cindy went to the grocery store, I pulled the spare mattress out of the basement. It was covered in a dusty sheet to keep it clean. I sneezed as I pulled the sheet off. It even smelled like the musty basement. I Febreezed the mattress and made up her spot in Ma's room for her. Ma had the largest room and, frankly, the only room that could hold another bed.

I found a plastic roll-away set of drawers in the basement and brought that up to Aunt Cindy's clothes. I decided to help her unpack. She had brought five pairs of shoes with her! She lived like a Hollywood queen. The shoes were heels of different colors. I dreamed that one day I would have more than two pairs of shoes- my hiking boots and my sneakers.

In her suitcase, I found an old picture of Grandma with Aunt Cindy and Ma as girls. Grandma looked beautiful with pin curls and a retro 70's style dress. Aunt Cindy and Ma looked about three and five. Everyone seemed so happy. It was a sweet picture.

Aunt Cindy returned from the grocery store and made her infamous shepherd's pie. It was deliciously made with ground lamb and topped with creamy, buttery mashed potatoes. The girls and I gobbled it down.

Aunt Cindy helped me wash up the girls after dinner. Then we watched some TV together while Aunt Cindy taught us schoolyard hand-clapping rhymes. We were all laughing and singing along and having a great time. It sure was nice to have some sense of normality back in the house. I felt like I hadn't smiled in weeks.

After a while, we all went to bed. I was still a little scared, but with Aunt Cindy at the house, I felt comfortable enough to sleep in my own bed. And I fell asleep faster than I had in a month.

It was about 3 am when I heard Aunt Cindy shriek. I ran into Ma's room to see what was the matter. Her covers were pulled back and a long black snake laid coiled in her bed. It was a gorgeous snake that had skin that looked like an oil slick. It was a common black king snake.

"There's a snake in my bed!" she cried.

"Aunt Cindy, it's just a garden snake," I said. Having grown up by the creek, Ma had taught me all about the different snakes so that I wouldn't fear them, but I knew which ones not to mess with. King snakes could be a bit snappy but they weren't venomous.

"I don't care what it is!" Aunt Cindy cried. "How are we going to get rid of it?"

"I'll get it," I said.

I carefully picked up the snake and took it outside, where it happily slithered away. Aunt Cindy was right behind me.

"How did it get in the house?" she asked.

"I don't know, Aunt Cindy," I said. "It's not really abnormal to see snakes around here. But there have been strange things happening in Ma's room."

I then proceeded to tell her everything that had happened while Ma was gone. And, for once, it seemed like somebody believed me.

"I don't know about all the other stuff, but I do know that it's not normal for a snake to crawl into your bed!" Aunt Cindy said. "Also, black snakes are bad luck. They represent dangerous enemies. I don't care if it's non venomous or not!"

"I mean, I guess we've never seen a snake actually in the house," I said with a yawn.

"Well, Charlotte, I think I will just sleep on the couch tonight," Aunt Cindy said. "We will discuss all this when your mom gets back tomorrow. Let's go back to bed."

"Okay, Aunt Cindy," I said. "Goodnight."

"Goodnight, Char," she said.

We went back into the house, and Aunt Cindy dragged her blanket and pillow to the living room. I couldn't wait for Ma to come home, and I couldn't wait for them to explain everything to me. Finally, I would get some answers.

Chapter 20

The next morning, Aunt Cindy was baking cinnamon rolls for breakfast.

"How did you sleep?" I asked.

"Not great at all!" Aunt Cindy said. "The couch was comfortable enough, but I couldn't shake the feeling of something slithering up my leg."

"Well, I didn't sleep good either," I said. "I haven't slept well in a while."

"I also could have sworn I heard you saying my name last night," she said. "But when I went to your room, you were passed out cold."

"I told you weird things have been happening around here," I said. "I am glad Ma will be back today."

"Yes, me, too," Aunt Cindy said. "Let's just make sure we don't badger her with questions and make her feel uncomfortable. It was a brave thing she did, asking for help. Sometimes asking for help can be the toughest thing in life."

"Gotcha," I responded.

"Now, let's eat some cinnamon rolls!" Aunt Cindy exclaimed.

We all ate cinnamon rolls and were getting dressed for the day when Ma walked in. She arrived earlier than planned. She seemed tired and a little distant, but she was in good spirits. The girls were sure happy to have her back home. And Aunt Cindy was overly excited to see her.

"Where have you been?" Anna demanded.

"Now, now," Aunt Cindy said. "Let's give your mom some space and time."

"It's okay, Cindy," Ma said. "I reckon I owe them an explanation." Ma sat down on the couch.

"Ya'll know I've been really stressed lately," she continued. "I just needed some time to think and to figure out what to do. That's why I called Aunt Cindy in for back-up."

"Like a reinforcement," Sadie asked, giggling.

"Yes, like a reinforcement here to save the day," Ma said.

"Oh, stop it," Aunt Cindy cried gleefully. "You know I wouldn't miss a good excuse to come to visit."

Aunt Cindy and Ma swapped childhood stories. And Aunt Cindy showed Ma the photo from their childhood. They talked about what it was like growing up in an eccentric household, whatever that meant. They laughed about memories, like the time that Ma was learning to ride a bike and stopped two lanes of traffic because she couldn't figure out how to use the breaks. They were having a grand ole time.

Aunt Cindy and Ma dug out sidewalk chalk and made a box in the driveway. Then, they found an old kickball in the basement. They showed us how to play an old game they used to play called four square. We had a blast.

While the girls and I played, Ma and Aunt Cindy did old cheers that they used to do in high school. Aunt Cindy was a few years younger than Ma but when she was a freshman, Ma was a senior and they got to both be on the cheer squad at the same time.

We all played Candyland together. Sadie won. Anna insisted she cheated as she usually did during board games. However, I was sure Sadie didn't because she had been on her best behavior since Aunt Cindy arrived. I think Sadie was possibly Aunt Cindy's favorite niece if she had one. Ma always had said Sadie and Aunt Cindy were a lot alike.

At dinner time, we prepped a large winter feast. Aunt Cindy and Ma taught me how to bake a turkey and ham. It was a lot easier than I thought. Ma made green bean casserole and mashed potatoes, and plenty of other side dishes. Aunt Cindy made an apple pie that smelled like heaven.

We all sat around the table, gorging on food. Aunt Cindy told us stories about Hollywood and living in Los Angeles. Sadie was amazed by Aunt Cindy's stories. Living in a big city seemed too noisy for me. I much preferred our small town and the peacefulness of the woods.

Once the girls got settled into bed that night, Aunt Cindy and Ma summoned me to the living room. Out on the table was the family Bible. Ma and Aunt Cindy sipped wine and gave me herbal tea. I waited for the highly anticipated conversation to start. Finally, Aunt Cindy began.

"So, from my understanding, you have pretty much figured out the spell of eternal life and what that means," Aunt Cindy started. "For centuries, our family practiced witchcraft. They used witchcraft for everyday work. They were bringing good luck, expelling negative energy, attracting love, and things of that nature. Well, a few generations back, they say that we turned to dark magic for more, eh, important matters such as becoming virtually immoral. Your great-grandmother, your grandmother, and even your mom used the spell of eternal life."

"Is that why both great-grandma and grandma are in such good health for their age?" I asked.

"We think so, but it's hard to be sure if it's that or just good genes," Aunt Cindy replied. "Your mom used the spell when she was 14. By the age of 18, your grandmother started diving more and more into the dark arts."

"And I wanted nothing to do with it," Ma chimed in. "That is why I haven't spoken to your grandmother in some time. As you girls got older, I couldn't risk her pushing her ways onto you. I put all of that behind me after your daddy died, and I became strictly Christian."

"But the family has always been Christian, right?" I asked.

"Well, the family was pagan until after the witch trials. Eventually, they became Christians but still used the craft," Ma said. "We believe that using the craft is the will of God, as long as you do not harm others."

"What about the demon?" I asked. "How does that come into play here?"

"Well, Charlotte, legend has it that if you don't complete the initiation by your 30th birthday, then he will come for your soul. We don't know if it's true or not, but if it is, that would explain all of the bad omens and strange things that have been taking place here."

"So, you practiced witchcraft when you were little?" I asked.

"Yes, I did," Ma said. "I grew up in witchcraft, so it's all I knew. All of my crystals are from when I still practiced. And when we used to pick wildflowers, that was a little bit of witchcraft. And I even made my teas using the craft."

"But if you weren't practicing dark magic, then why did you stop?" I asked.

"I *did* practice dark magic when I used the spell of eternal life," Ma said. "When I noticed Grandma going down a darker and darker path, that's when I decided to leave the craft altogether. I didn't want to spiral out of control as she did."

"Is this why you have so many superstitions?" I asked.

Aunt Cindy laughed, "Yes, that is why most in the family are superstitious, but your mom has just always been that way.

"What does any of this have to do with the clearing? Why did you stop going to the clearing?" I asked Ma.

"The clearing is where the family picked wildflowers for spells. It is also where we spent time completing rituals," Ma said. "That is where your grandmother completed the Eternal Life spell and had her initiation. I feel like that made the clearing unsafe."

"So, what do we do now?" I asked. "Why are you telling me this now."

"Charlotte, witchcraft is what brought these things upon us, and it's what will send these things away," Ma said. "Your Aunt Cindy is here to help us. But I am afraid that us two alone won't be strong enough to expel the evil that has surrounded me."

I just stared blankly at Ma.

"We are going to need your help," she said.

"Really?!" I said excitedly.

I couldn't put a finger on it, but I was thrilled to be able to help. Perhaps it was engaging in my family's rich history that excited me so.

"Yes. We will also be asking Sarah and Bobby to join us," Ma said.

"Does Sarah know what we are doing?" I asked Ma.

"No, and she can't know until she gets here, or she would probably never agree to come," Ma said. "Sarah is Southern Baptist born and raised, and she would never understand, much less believe us. But I need her here to help make sure the girls are safe when we get started."

"Why does Bobby have to come?" I sighed.

"Charlotte, I know you don't like Bobby, but he is a good man," Ma said.

"And we might need a little muscle."

"I know. Bobby came by while you were gone to replace the dryer belt," I confessed. "He was really nice to me. I did tell him you were gone, so I am sure he will be happy you're back since he's got a big ole crush on you!"

Ma and Aunt Cindy both burst out into laughter.

"So, what will I be doing?" I asked.

"You will be helping your Aunt Cindy with a counterspell to break the spell of eternal life," Ma said. "I am going to need you to be brave. If there really is a demonic force at play here, it could get horrific. I know you are strong, but it could get scary. However, hopefully, it will put an end to everything we have been experiencing."

"Okay," I said. "When do we start?"

"We are starting tomorrow night during the full moon. It's when our energy and powers will be strongest," Aunt Cindy said promptly.

"I don't have powers," I said.

"Of course you do," Aunt Cindy exclaimed. "We all have powers inside of us. We just have to choose to use them. And that's why you need a good night's rest."

"And you must take a bath in an oil I have made for you," Ma said. "It is an oil made with lavender, eucalyptus, rosemary, and lemon to help purify you as well as put you to sleep. We will all be taking a bath tonight."

"So, off to bed you go," Aunt Cindy said.

"Oh, wait," Ma said. "I just wanted to say I am sorry, Charlotte. It's not an excuse, but if there is a demon attacking me, it has no doubt been draining my energy. That would explain why I have been so depressed and unable to get over your dad."

"And why have you been lashing out?" I asked.

"Yes, that, too," Ma said, embarrassed.

"Demons suck the positivity and joy out of a person," Aunt Cindy butted in. "It can make them irrational and moody. I am sure your mom will be better once we resolve this issue. Now, off to your bath and bed."

I gave them each a hug goodnight and headed to take a bath. I ran the water and put a few drops of the oil in. I slid into the tub and let the water soothe me. I washed every inch of skin and thought about everything they had told me.

I was glad I wasn't crazy and that I had been right. I could finally breathe a breath of relief. And knowing that Ma would be better soon was promising. But I was still unsettled by the fact that a demonic entity was at the root of all this.

I finished my bath and put on a comfy pair of pajamas. I wasn't sure how I was supposed to fall asleep with all the excitement. But nearly as soon as my head hit the pillow, I was fast asleep.

Chapter 21

The next day, we spent the day preparing. Ma brought up the box from the attic. She pulled out the flower bundles.

"What are these for?" I asked.

"They are for smoke cleansing," Ma said. "The smoke helps get rid of evil spirits. Our Scottish ancestors used to burn herbs and flowers for protection and other things like attracting positive energy. Now, help me clear out the living room, so we have space."

I cleared out the living room. I moved the coffee table. And I pulled up the rug. I also removed any breakable items from the living room. As Ma said, that was the safest route.

Ma created a large pentagram in the middle of the floor with her quartz crystals and obsidian stones. She said it was for protection. She then put candles up around the living room in case the power was to go out. She made an anointing oil with licorice root oil and dried sunflower petals. She insisted we all rub some on our temples and collarbones to help keep us safe while also making us stronger.

Aunt Cindy created what she believed was a spell to reverse the eternal life spell. She wrote it down and placed it in the family Bible. It read:

Enemy of mine, your power is gone.
The deal is broken, the spell undone.
Astorath you've gone away.
So you shall be from this day.
This spell is cast,
This spell will last.

Astorath, I rebuke thee,
This is my will, so mote it be!

She had me help gather black and red candles, a crow feather, and bay leaves. She had a printed copy of the Prayer to Saint Michael to protect us. And we were all set to go.

First, Bobby came over.

"Well, Luna, I don't believe in this hocus pocus, but I'll do whatever you need me to do," Bobby said.

"Thank you, Bobby," Ma said. "I just need you to help out if Charlotte and Cindy need some strength.

"You got it, pretty lady," Bobby said.

Next, Sarah arrived.

"Listen, Sarah. I think a demonic element is tormenting me," Ma said. "And we are going to try to banish it. I think I might be cursed."

"Luna, this isn't right," Anna said. "I don't believe in this stuff, and even if it did, it goes against everything I believe in. Witchcraft is evil, and I can't have any part in it. I think you are just stressed and depressed, Luna."

"Sarah, I am asking you to please help me," Ma said. "I am desperate."

Sarah sighed and looked at the floor at her feet. "Okay, Luna. But if this doesn't work, you have to seek professional help. I think you're just stressed and still grieving. Grief is a powerful emotion, and everybody grieves differently."

"Deal," Ma said. "If this doesn't work, I will go see a psychiatrist."

We finished getting ready, and then Ma had me take the girls out for some fresh air and tell them what to expect.

"Sadie. Anna," I said. "I need to talk to you. So let's go swing for a while."

We went outside, and both the girls hopped on a swing. I alternated pushing them while they sang in the winter breeze.

"What did you want to talk to us about?" Sadie finally asked.

I stood there for a moment, thinking of how to explain everything to two small children.

"Ma needs our help tonight," I said. "It could get a little scary, but I need you two to be brave."

"What does she need help with?" Anna asked.

"She needs help getting better," I continued. "Ma has been very sad, so we are going to help her."

"What's scary about that?" Sadie asked.

I stood there, again. Ma said not to tell them too many details but to tell them enough to be prepared.

"Ma has a curse on her," I said. "So we are going to break the curse. And some weird things could happen."

"Like when my music box was playing by itself," Sadie said.

"Yes, just like that," I told her. "But we are going to be brave. Okay? And you are just going to do whatever Miss Sarah tells you to do, okay?"

"Okay," they both chimed.

I spent the rest of the day playing with the girls as Ma talked to the adults. I didn't want the girls to eavesdrop and stress about the evening. They would be in their room with Miss Sarah, but I was still worried about them.

I would die if anything happened to them. Over the last couple of years of taking care of them, I felt like I was responsible for the girls. They were a part of my soul and my reasons for living. It was like they were my children, even though I knew it probably wasn't healthy to feel that way.

I imagined Ma getting better and being back to her happy self like before Daddy died. I wondered if I would still help take care of the girls. We had a routine down, and I knew what the girls liked to play and do. I wasn't sure if Ma would be ready to relearn what the girls wanted.

And what about me? While I was tired of being treated like the household's caretaker, I couldn't imagine being treated like a child again. I also wondered if Ma and I could genuinely mend our relationship. She had said sorry to me a couple of times lately, but I still felt some sense of awkwardness with her. Ma was very codependent on me, and I couldn't imagine life any other way.

At the end of the day, though, we would have to face all of that when the time came. I was just ready and excited to have Ma back. Perhaps this was going to be the fresh start that we all needed.

Ma made a fire in the fire pit in the backyard. She insisted that she must burn her journal so that Aunt Cindy could use the ashes in the counterspell.

So, we all huddled around the fire pit as we watched it burn. I looked at Ma and wondered if she knew that I had read her diary.

Since we were starting fresh, I decided to go get my journal to burn as well. I would no longer need to write down my negative thoughts. I was confident, too, that I shouldn't keep reminders of the past two years around. So I headed to my room.

While in my room, I heard Sadie's music box begin to play. I went to her room and, sure enough, it was playing. For a few moments, I nervously watched the ballerina spend around and around. Then, I quickly shut the box and headed out of there.

When I made it down the hall to my room, my radio began blasting "Paint It Black" by The Rolling Stones. I shut it off as fast as I could. Then, I felt a rush of air blew against my face and was left breathless. I felt a hand grab my arm, and I screamed.

"Ma!" I cried.

"I'm sorry, Charlotte," Ma said. "I didn't mean to frighten you!"

"It's okay," I said with a relieved sigh. "Sadie's music box was playing again, and my radio turned on by itself."

"Well, hopefully, this ends tonight," Ma said. She took my hand and looked at me with softness in her eyes. "It is time."

Chapter 22

Night fell, and after dinner, we wasted no time in getting started. Miss Sarah set up the TV in the girls' room to watch a movie together and stay out of the way. We all rubbed anointing oil on ourselves and then got ready to go.

Aunt Cindy, Ma, Bobby, and I got inside the crystal pentagram and held hands. Aunt Cindy began to read the Prayer of St Michael:

St. Michael the Archangel,

defend us in battle.

Be our defense against the wickedness and snares of the Devil.

May God rebuke him, we humbly pray,

and do thou,

O Prince of the heavenly hosts,

by the power of God,

thrust into hell Satan,

and all the evil spirits,

who prowl about the world

seeking the ruin of souls. Amen.

At the same time that she said amen, the electricity went out. I flinched. And I could hear the girls startled in their room.

"Stay strong and do not break the circle," Ma said.

I swallowed real hard and grasped onto their hands a little firmer. Aunt Cindy began reciting the counterspell, and Ma began to scream. Suddenly, her body went almost lifeless, and her eyes glazed over.

In a deep, other-worldly voice, she said, "For you cannot escape. Necesse est aut imiteris aut oderis."

Then she started coughing horrendously. Aunt Cindy was patting her on the back when suddenly and violently, wildflowers began spewing out of her mouth uncontrollably. Her mouth was opened wider than should be humanly possible. I thought she might choke to death.

Her body bent over backward in a way that only a contortionist would be able to bend, and we broke the circle. When her body snapped straight, she said in that same voice, "You cannot get rid of me, *wildflower witches*. For you have a due to pay."

It was at that moment that Ma went flying backward, and she slammed into a wall.

Blood was dripping from her nose. Her face was pale and clammy while her veins were protruding under her skin.

Aunt Cindy said, "Get back inside the pentagram, Charlotte."

She began repeating the Prayer of Saint Michael. Ma screamed out in agony. Tears that were as dark as night and looked like oil began to flow down her cheeks as she spewed more wildflowers. I was trembling.

Then Ma said, "I have never loved you, Charlotte. I will never love you; you spoiled brat." I began to cry.

"Charlotte, don't listen. That is the demon talking. Your mother loves you very much. Think of a happy memory with her," Aunt Cindy said.

The candlelights flickered until they all went out, and the windows burst into a million shattered pieces. A horrifying scene of Ma running across the floor on all fours and then up the wall and onto the ceiling ensued. She jumped down and landed on all fours like a cat. Her hair was hanging wildly in her face as she groaned and growled. Then she let out a horrifying shriek that sounded like a demented creature.

Then Aunt Cindy was pushed by an invisible force and flung across the room into the couch. I forced myself to think about Ma and me dipping our toes in the stream and picking wildflowers. I stepped out of the circle.

"Charlotte, it's not safe out of the pentagram!" Aunt Cindy yelled.

"Aunt Cindy, it's not safe *in* the pentagram," I said.

I took Ma's wrists, and I grasped them tightly.

"Ma, listen to me. You must fight this. The girls love you. Aunt Cindy loves you. I love you," I said.

For a moment, Ma was still.

"Help me, Bobby! We can bind her to a kitchen chair," I said.

Bobby placed Ma in a chair, and I grabbed duct tape from below the kitchen sink. We taped her to the chair the best that we could. Then Aunt Cindy proceeded with the spell.

Ma hissed and growled.

"You stupid bitch, you can't get rid of me," she said in that same terrifying voice. Her pupils and irises were so tiny that most of her eyes were white. She was sweating profusely. She spat at Aunt Cindy.

Aunt Cindy just read louder and faster as Ma spewed horrid profanities.

"Charlotte, I need you to help me and read this as loud as you can," Aunt Cindy cried.

So in unison, we read the spell. Aunt Cindy threw wildflowers at Ma's feet and splashed her with the anointing oil that Ma had made earlier in the day. I burned the wildflower bundles. She screamed. We kept chanting the spell over and over until suddenly it went quiet.

"I love you, Charlotte," Ma said. "I love Anna and Sadie, too."

Ma passed out. Aunt Cindy quickly unbound her and laid her on the floor.

"Quick, Bobby, call 9-1-1," Aunt Cindy said. "I can't feel a pulse."

I cried by Ma's side as she laid there lifelessly. The girls came into the living room, and we all embraced Ma, crying.

"Wake up, Ma," Anna said.

"It's okay, girls," I tried to console them.

Before too long, paramedics arrived. Aunt Cindy had us stand out of the way while they put Ma on a stretcher. We all stood crying as they rolled Ma out the door. I hugged the girls as the ambulance siren wailed, and emergency lights filled the living room through the broken window.

Aunt Cindy didn't want to leave us, so she sent Bobby to the hospital to be with Ma. We cleaned up the broken glass and boarded up the windows to keep the cold out. We put away the items that we used for the spell. I put the living room back together. We tried to make everything normal again.

Miss Sarah stayed with us all night long as we waited by the telephone for Bobby to call. She mostly looked after the girls. She kept them preoccupied and entertained so that they wouldn't worry too much. Aunt Cindy and I just silently sat on the couch.

It was about 6 am and the sun was barely coming up when the phone rang. "Hello?" I answered.

"Hi, Charlotte," Bobby said. "Can you put your Aunt Cindy on the phone?"

"Is Ma okay?" I asked.

"Char, just put your aunt on the phone, please," Bobby said.

"Aunt Cindy," I called for her. "It's Bobby. He wants to speak to you."

I tried to eavesdrop, but I could hear anything. After a couple of moments of silence, Aunt Cindy let the phone drop from her hand, and she slid down the wall crying. Tears filled my eyes. Now, I knew what the news was.

"Your momma said she loves you very much, Charlotte," Aunt Cindy consoled me. "She felt awful for everything that had happened."

"I know she did," I said.

We just sat on the floor and held each other, crying for what seemed an eternity.

Chapter 23

Ma's funeral was a week later, and it was beautiful. The entire town had gotten together and brought her wildflowers of all kinds, as requested by Aunt Cindy. The girls and I were all dressed in black. Aunt Cindy had insisted that I wear the sapphire cloak, so I did.

I silently cried as they laid her on the ground. The girls and I each threw in a Virginia bluebell.

Grandma came to the funeral, but she stayed quietly in the back, and she left as soon as it was over. Aunt Cindy said that it was to respect Ma's wishes. Ma hadn't wanted us, children, to be a part of her life, so she respected that wish. But she looked beautiful. Her hair was white as snow, but she looked barely older than Ma. She had worn a black dress with a shimmering black cloak and ruby red lipstick. I wish I could have at least said hello to her. She couldn't be that bad. Alas, though, Ma's wishes were to be respected.

They say that Ma's heart just stopped just as Daddy's had. Aunt Cindy believes that Ma just missed Daddy so much that she couldn't bear the pain of living without him anymore. And when they broke the Eternal Life spell, Ma had her greatest wish of all— to be with Daddy again.

I was sad, but I was also glad that Ma wouldn't be suffering anymore. Seeing her so depressed the last couple of years had broken me in ways that I never thought possible. And I knew that Ma loved us, girls. She was just hurting.

Speaking of the girls, they were sad, but they were holding up much better than I expected. They had only cried the night Ma died. And other than the funeral, they were acting like themselves. I was worried that we were going to go into foster care now, though. Child Protection Services would never let me take care of them as I am too young.

"What happens now?" I asked Aunt Cindy as we drove home from the funeral.

"What do you mean?" she asked.

"I mean, who is going to take care of us?" I asked. "I can take care of the girls, but I don't think Dottie is going to let that happen."

"Don't be silly, Charlotte," Aunt Cindy said. "I am going to take care of you, of course."

"You are?" I asked with my eyes lighting up. I knew Aunt Cindy cared about us, but I never expected her to leave her Hollywood life behind.

"What will you do? I thought you were waiting on your big break," I said.

"Well, I was," Aunt Cindy said. "But Hollywood isn't going anywhere. And, truthfully, it's time for me to take a little break."

"So, are we living with you?" I asked.

"No, no. I am moving in with *you*," Aunt Cindy said as she booped my nose. I giggled for the first time in a week.

"The house has been in the family for generations, Charlotte," she said. "As oldest, it is to be passed on to you when you become of age. So we will live in your house for the time being; until you are ready to go off to college or whatever it is that you wish to do."

We made it home, and we began to clean out Ma's room. Aunt Cindy insisted that I stay in Ma's room now since it was my house. We got rid of her old clothes and belongings. I moved my things into her room. But I did keep her crystals and the wildflowers. I would always keep the wildflowers.

It was weird sitting in the same bed that Ma had spent so much time in. I imagined her sitting there with a romance novel in one hand and a cigarette in the other. Speaking of which, I needed to clean the walls and furniture as it smelled like stale cigarettes in Ma's room.

I looked around the room and thought of all the weird things that had happened in this space. It had only been a week, but it seemed like a lifetime ago. All the hauntings and strange things stopped after the night that Ma died.

I hadn't been too distraught over Ma dying. I did miss her and was sad. But I felt like I had gotten the closure I needed. I knew that Ma loved me and appreciated me. And I knew that she was probably just ready to be with Daddy again.

It was still peculiar to have the house so peaceful. Without Ma's lashing out and the hauntings, it would almost be too quiet if it weren't for Aunt Cindy. Aunt Cindy had shown us lots of love and patience. It was like she was made to have children. She knew how to be playful and carefree. She was also encouraging and approachable. Aside from Ma passing, life was actually kind of good. And it was time to move forward.

Chapter 24

I t is ten years later.

I am filling the bookshelves of my bookstore. After college, I got a business loan and came back to Billington to fulfill my lifelong dream. I am officially a bookstore owner, and I will have my grand opening in two weeks. It is called "Luna's Shelves."

It's a small bookstore on the corner across the Piggly Wiggly in town. It is warmly lit, with industrial lights hanging low from the ceiling. It has real wooden bookshelves with leather lounges. It smells of oak and leather. It feels like my calling.

Anna and Sadie are each in high school now. But they moved off to California, where Aunt Cindy put them in a fancy art school. Sadie is interested in theater, and Anna loved photography. Aunt Cindy had her big break, after all. And she could give the girls a life they could have only dreamed about.

I studied religion in college. I picked up the family's old ways, using wildflowers in my craft. I didn't go to church, but I prayed daily. I wore Ma's antique sapphire pendant around my neck.

I was thinking about how great life had turned out. Then, in walks a beautiful woman with dark chocolate brown hair and big, gorgeous brown eyes. Her skin is a warm tan color. I am awestruck. I don't know her, but she seems familiar.

"I'm not open quite yet," I smile at the woman.

"Oh, I am not here for a book," the woman warmly says. "I am here to speak to Charlotte Wardwell."

"Well, that's me," I said. "What can I do for ya?"

"I need your help," she said. "I am Olivia Garcia. I spoke to my Aunt Sarah, and she said you could help me. My brother's house is not well. We think it's possessed."

"I am not sure how I can help," I said with a sigh. "Have you considered going to the church?"

"Yes, we went to the church," she said. "They sent us to Blytown to the Catholic Church. The priest said that he could not help us without consent from the Vatican, and he said there isn't enough evidence even to submit our case in a request."

"I am sorry to hear that, but the last time I got involved with something like this, someone died," I told her.

"I know. It was your mother who died," Olivia said. "But, I am desperate."

I remembered Ma saying those very words to Sarah. Sarah had helped us even when she didn't want to. Sarah had even risked her own life to help us. Maybe I owed it to Sarah to help her niece and nephew.

"Okay, I will help you," I said reluctantly. "But we are doing things my way even if they're a little, uh, unorthodox."

"Thank you so much," Olivia said. "You have no idea how much this means to me. And, yes, I am aware that you are a witch? Is that what you mean by unorthodox?"

I replied, "Yep. I am a *wildflower witch*."

"Well, I see no problem with that," Olivia said warmly.

We chatted for about thirty minutes about Olivia's brother, Charlie. She explained everything that had been happening, and I listened carefully. It definitely sounded like they needed some help, so I was set out to do my best. After all, wildflower witches are strong.

Manufactured by Amazon.ca
Bolton, ON

21084621R00074